DAUGHTERS OF THE SUN

and other stories

Also by Obi Egbuna

The Anthill
(a play)

OBI EGBUNA

Daughters of the Sun
and other stories

London

OXFORD UNIVERSITY PRESS

New York   Ibadan   Nairobi

1970

Oxford University Press, Ely House, London W. 1

GLASGOW   NEW YORK   TORONTO   MELBOURNE   WELLINGTON
CAPE TOWN   SALISBURY   IBADAN   NAIROBI   DAR ES SALAAM   LUSAKA   ADDIS ABABA
BOMBAY   CALCUTTA   MADRAS   KARACHI   LAHORE   DACCA
KUALA LUMPUR   SINGAPORE   HONG KONG   TOKYO

SBN 19 211361 5

© Oxford University Press 1970

Printed in Great Britain
by Lowe & Brydone (Printers) Ltd., London

CONTENTS

DIVINITY

The cock was crowing in the distance. The wind moaned ominously outside the Mission gates. Catechist Thomas was in his parlour loading a gun. He was much disturbed and angry. A lean, ageing man, he had long slender hands and long trembling fingers. You could tell from his scraggy neck and overworked Adam's apple that he was a preacher. In spite of his fast-greying hair and other outward signs of age, he looked remarkably energetic, tough, and resolute. Balanced on the bridge of his dilated black nose was an old pair of spectacles with one arm of the frame missing. He wore a striped pyjama top, which was now converted into a shirt, a pair of tropical-khaki trousers held in place by broad brown braces, and on his feet were thick tyre-soled slippers. That the old man had long staked his hopes on the furniture of Heaven could be seen by the scanty furnishing of the room: a few wooden chairs arranged on the floor mat. Overhead was a bamboo ceiling and through open blindless windows one could almost see the sun's rays enacting photo-synthesis with the palm leaves. The cement walls, like the ceiling, were whitewashed and carried biblical pictures here and there, and an old crucifix. Suddenly drum and tom-tom beats began sounding down in the village. The old man started, laid down his gun, listened, lips compressed. His eyes reddened like a setting sun. Now the drums sounded loud and near, now they seemed distant and faint. Occasionally, the sound of elephant-tusk horn tore through the air. And then, as suddenly as it had started, the whole weird noise stopped again. The old man's nerves relaxed once more like the loosened string of a bow. He picked up his gun and started wiping it again, grinding his teeth like a drill on hard rock.

Rapid knocks sounded on the door.

'Who's there?' he roared, snatching up the gun.

1

'It's only me, father,' answered a younger voice. 'Let me in. Quickly.'

'Oh, it's you, David,' said the catechist with relief. 'What d'you want?'

'To talk to you, father.'

'But I told you I wasn't to be disturbed until I've got the gun ready.'

'That's what I want to talk to you about, father.' David's voice sounded urgent. 'I've just come down from the village. You must listen to me. Please!'

The old man sighed.

'All right,' he said reluctantly. 'The door's open.'

David was a handsome boy, of nearly twenty-one. Strikingly tall in spotless white shirt, well-ironed dark trousers, his college tie and a pair of pointed black shoes, he made his father look medieval by contrast. His hair was shiny black, low-cut, and parted thinly in the middle. Apart from a tiny yellow scar on his forehead which he had borne since the day he slipped and hit his head on the board while competing in the triple jump at the college last sports season, he had a smooth, long, baby-like face which tapered into a black, fibrous, cone-shaped goatee. He came into the room, shutting the door cautiously and sat on the edge of the table. He opened his mouth but seemed to have difficulty in starting.

'Well?' said his father impatiently. 'I'm running short of time, you know. So make it snappy.'

'You sound snappy all right,' David joked feebly, his nervous chuckle betraying fear rather than amusement.

'I'm in no laughing mood, David.'

'Who can't see that, blindfolded?'

'What d'you want?'

David cleared his throat and began warily:

'Surely, father, you're not going through with this, are you?'

'Lord have mercy on us!' the catechist sniffed in disgust. 'We're not going through all that again.'

2

'D'you expect me to stay here and let you commit what's virtually suicide?'

'My dear son, far greater men than I have sacrificed their lives for less noble causes than this. This is the eternal truth of the good book. And it will always be.'

'But why does it have to be you this time, father?'

'Because I'm the catechist in this parish, that's why,' the old man shouted. 'I'm doing what the Almighty Designer requires of His humble servant. So help me God!'

'Does God require you to fight a whole village single-handed?'

'He commands us all to fight evil in all its phases. The Ozo-Ebunu Society is an evil circle, the worst terrorist organization one can possibly conceive. I'll break them tonight or perish in the attempt.'

'It's the oldest institution in the land, father.'

'By the time I'm finished with them tonight, it'll be the dirtiest thing that ever happened in this village and the latest to vanish. I swear it, David —'

The tom-tom began to thump again in the distance, filling the air with terror.

'Can you hear that, father?' David whispered. 'The tom-tom says you're walking straight into the jaws of a crocodile.'

'This time the crocodile has bitten off more than it can chew.'

'That's what I'm afraid of, father. These people have always bitten off more than they can chew. And then chew it!'

'How do you mean: and then they chew it?'

'You know what became of those who defied Divinity, don't you?'

'Stop calling the Juju 'Divinity', will you?' shouted the old man angrily. 'You talk as if you were one of them. The Juju is no more a spirit than that Aladdin lamp on the table.'

'Father, please lower your voice.' David was frightened.

'I don't care who hears me. I've said it before and I'll say it again. I'm here to bear witness to the Lord. Anyone who calls

3

Juju a spirit is a blasphemer against the Almighty Designer.' He made the sign of the cross every time he referred to the Almighty Designer. 'I'll expose them once and for all tonight.'

'Father,' David began, 'many years ago, a man wanted to expose them once and for all. But instead of disproving the divinity of the Juju, his own body was found at the bottom of the river.'

'Nonsense! That was a fabricated nonsense designed to scare spineless people out of their wits and intimidate them into joining the black ring. Well, son, your father isn't so spineless.'

'What about seven years ago when a woman member of the circle revealed their secret while she was drunk? Remember what became of her?'

'That's a good reason why the society must be swept from the face of God's earth. The kidnapper must be exposed.'

'And don't forget. Only a couple of years ago, the Juju was dancing at Olisa Square when the District Commissioner's clerk threw a spear at it. The man went home to find that very spear driven through the heart of his own daughter. And, around her heart, a black circle, the mark of the Ozo-Ebunu Society.'

'Another foul trick, I tell you!'

'And what about the American tourist who had a bet with them and shot at the Juju from the top of a tree? He dropped dead himself, didn't he? And with a bullet through his own heart and of course the usual black ring round the wound? Nothing happened to the Juju. Is that not a proof that this thing has some divine power after all?'

'Shut up, David!' shouted the old man. 'I refuse to hear my own son talking like a non-Catholic. Your mother and I — may God rest her dear soul — your mother and I brought you up in the Christian faith. And you were a good boy, went to Mass regularly, received your communion, served at Mass, said your prayers constantly, and for three consecutive years won the prize for being the best chorister of the year; you did everything a good boy should do, and I was the proudest father in the land, till two years

4

ago when you won that scholarship and got into the University only to involve yourself with that — what do you call it? — Black Power Society. All this negritude business! Huh!'

'Oh — I give up.' David fidgeted impatiently. 'Why does all this have to happen just when I'm home on holiday?'

The catechist patted him on the back.

'Sorry about that, son,' he said softly, and then added firmly: 'But what must be must be!'

'Even if it means your death? I'm worried for you, father. You're the only person I've left in this world since Mamma died. Supposing they kill you tonight? What am I going to do?'

'Nothing will happen to your father, son,' said the catechist affectionately. 'God is on our side. Remember what the Lord said: With faith in Him, a man can move mountains.'

'Father, the Ozo-Ebunu Society is not a mountain. From what they say, it is nothing short of a sub-planet on earth.'

'Is that the best encouragement you can give to your father at a time like this?'

'I'm sorry, father. But we must face facts. Oh, how can I convince you to be reasonable?'

'By doing what?'

'Just what they asked. Give them what they want.'

'What? A basket of kola nuts and a goat? And a verbal apology on top of it all?'

'An apology won't kill you, father. After all, humility is a cardinal Christian virtue.'

'It's not as simple as that, David. It's a matter of principle. Besides, it's too late. The world knows about it already. Every newspaper printer is sitting up tonight to see what will happen. To give up now means that they're right, and I, and all I stand for, are wrong. No, David, my mind's made up.'

'Then let me apologize for you, father. There's still time. It's never too late as long as one's still breathing.'

'I won't hear of it! Take back what I said? Ha! Over my dead body!'

5

'That's what I'm afraid of, father. It might just happen over your dead body.'

'Let's consider this conversation closed,' said the catechist, rising from his seat.

'As you wish, father.'

The old man put the gun safely in the corner. He collected a badly worn coat which was hanging behind the bedroom door, and then his hat. Putting these on, he opened a wooden chest from which he took his rosary. Finally, he picked up his walking stick and hurried towards the door.

'If anyone wants me,' he said, opening the door, 'I've gone to ring the angelus.'

'And after that, your mid-day rosary, I suppose?'

'Of course.' Catechist Thomas slammed the door behind him.

David shook his head despondently. He walked back to the table, picked up a copy of a Catholic magazine, read a few lines, and flung the periodical back onto the table, exclaiming, 'Huh!'

Someone knocked on the door.

'Who is it?' called David as the door swung open. A bald-headed white man came in. He wore a white cassock and a patronizing smile.

'Hello, David,' said the priest, his accent Irish to the last lilt.

'Father Galligan!' exclaimed David. 'This is a pleasant surprise. Won't you come in?'

'Thank you, David. How nice to see you. On holiday, are you? Well now, where's your father, the good Thomas?'

Just then, as if in answer to the question, the angelus began to chime. They exchanged smiles, bowed their heads, and prayed. Prayer over, they sat down.

'I was just going to tell you where father was,' said David smiling, 'but the old man has his ways of speaking up for himself.'

'Yes, so I gather.' Father Galligan laughed.

'If it's something urgent, I'll have to go for him. I'm afraid he won't be back till he's said his mid-day rosary.'

'No,' said Father Galligan with a wave of his hand, 'don't

6

disturb him. But,' he added with a frown, 'it's something urgent all right.'

'Oh dear! Can I help?'

'I don't know. I got a telegram this morning. No signature. It says your father's in grave trouble.'

'I see,' David grunted reflectively. 'I'm glad someone cares.'

'And when I was coming through the village just now,' the priest continued, 'I sensed something sinister in the air. Usually I can hardly jostle my way up here through the crowd of villagers, all laughing and greeting me. But today, the whole place is deserted and quiet. Not a soul in sight. See — my pockets are still bulging with the bars of chocolate I usually give away. It was like driving through a valley of fear.'

'Valley of fear!' David echoed. 'The understatement of the year, I assure you.'

'Has your father anything to do with it?'

'Anything to do with it! He's the cause of it.'

'What's he done?'

'He's decided to wage war against the Ozo-Ebunu Society single-handed.'

'Ozo-Ebunu,' repeated Father Galligan with effort. 'Let me see now. You mean the —'

'Surely, Father, you've heard about the Juju circle, haven't you?'

'Well, only some vague whisperings here and there. And I know that His Grace's penalty for any Christian who has anything to do with the secret society is instant excommunication. That's about all I do know. People are usually frightened to death to talk about it. Even in the town where I live, the freedom of the press automatically ceases to exist when it comes to this Juju affair. They never report their murders. The churchwarden once told me that it wouldn't surprise him if the editors themselves were secret members of the society.'

'Nonsense!' retorted David. 'You mustn't listen to such rumours.'

7

'I must admit I didn't give it much credence at the time. But never mind — tell me more about it.'

'There's not much to tell, really,' David answered. 'I don't know much about it myself. Nobody knows exactly how the society originated. The members claim that the Juju, which they call Divinity, incidentally, has always existed and always will. The minimum age for membership is twenty for men and twenty-five for women. They take an oath on admission. And, with them, an oath is an oath. To obey all the rules; never to divulge a single secret — if they do, the penalty is death; and above all, to accept and advocate the immortality, the omnipotence, the omniscience, the omnipresence — in short, the absolute divinity of the Juju."

'What does the Juju look like?'

'Indescribable, Father. Unless an important member of the group dies, the Juju comes out only once a year. And this takes six whole months to prepare. And when it does appear, people come from all parts to see it, give their donations, and ask Divinity's blessings. It's almost as tall as a palm tree. One hardly dares look at its face.'

'Then it's a masquerade of some sort?'

'Father Galligan,' replied David, looking about him cautiously, 'I don't think it's safe to answer that question. Let me just tell you what an American reporter once wrote about it in a magazine. He said the Juju is a "swell work of art, raffia embroidery, and terrorism complex." What d'you think of that?'

The priest laughed.

'An apt description indeed,' he said, noting that David was not in the least amused.

'Surely, Father,' he heard him say, 'purely from the artistic point of view, it's beautiful and —'

'Very fine, I'm sure. Very very fine. Tell me, David, what exactly does this Juju do when it comes out?'

'Oh, dances, sways, sings, and the henchmen chant in response. And as they dance, no one, not even the oldest member, is allowed to go within six yards of him.'

8

'You seem to know a lot about it, David?'

'Oh, only as an aesthetic experience, Father. I wrote a paper about it for our African Cultural Society at the University. I'm Vice-Chairman, you know.'

'No, I didn't know. But how did your father get himself involved in this Juju business then?'

'If the Archbishop hadn't declared this the Anti-Superstition Year, all this would not have started.'

Father Galligan chuckled.

'So, you're blaming it all on His Grace!' he said.

'Well, it's true, Father Galligan. Since the anti-superstition announcement, my father has been all out against the Juju. He's attacked the society three times from the pulpit. And three times they've warned him through our family head to stop it. They sent him what we call Admonition Kola Nut. In spite of this, my father attacked the Juju again last Sunday.'

'And so?'

'They've decided not to let him go this time. They gave him five days to apologize to the Juju through our family head. And, to abate Divinity's anger, he must donate the Juju a basket of kola nuts and a goat.'

'And what's your father going to do about it?'

'He says he's neither apologizing nor giving them anything.'

'So what's the position now?'

'The deadline is midnight tonight. If my father doesn't comply with their wishes then, the Juju and the henchmen are coming here in person to demand their due.'

'And what if your father refuses to apologize?'

'Please don't ask me, Father,' said David, looking down, frightened. 'I can't bear to think of it.'

'St. Patrick!' exclaimed the priest with horrified expression. 'That would be murder.'

'My father has got his gun loaded. He says he won't let them come as close as our house. He's going to wait for them somewhere down in the araba bushes by the hillside. He reckons to shoot the

9

Juju down. That way, he hopes to explode the myth of the Juju's divinity once and for all.'

'Good man!' exclaimed Father Galligan in grim jubilation.

'Good man!' repeated David, obviously stunned. 'Surely you aren't going to let him do anything so plainly suicidal?'

'How do you mean: suicidal?'

'Haven't you heard of what happened to other people who attempted to destroy the Juju in the past? They ended up destroying themselves. The Juju is still going strong today, isn't it?'

'Nonsense!' said the priest impatiently. 'You surprise me, David. I'm disappointed that a university undergraduate of your intellectual calibre should countenance such superstitious humbug. The Juju's only a raffia mask which, according to your palm-tree description, must be quite heavy and sweaty for the poor fellow who puts it on.'

'Supposing you're right, Father, supposing it's only a mask worn by a man, won't it be sheer cold-blooded murder for my father to shoot that man tonight?'

'But they are coming to do just that to your father!'

'Two wrongs don't make a right, Father Galligan. Certainly not according to the Christian teaching.'

'If God Himself struck down Saul to make St Paul out of him, how can he not approve of your father striking down one heathen to make Christians out of many?'

'And if the heathen strikes him down instead and makes "Judases" out of the "Thomases" of the Church today, what then?'

'Then it will have been an enviable failure after an attempt. Your father will have accomplished a martyr's death worthy of a catechist of God. And this village which, up till now, has had only the temerity to produce a Juju, will have had the opportunity to give humanity a saint. Can't you see the sanctity of your father's decision?'

'It's the sanity that puzzles me, Father.'

They both began to laugh and were about to abandon the subject for something less argumentative when a rap sounded on

10

the door.

'Come in,' David called out. The door half opened and the head of a young man appeared.

'Oh, am I interrupting anything?' he stuttered.

'Hello, Danny Boy,' said David. 'Step right in.'

'Thanks.'

'Oh, Father Galligan,' David continued, 'you know my cousin, Daniel. We are at university together.'

'Good afternoon, Father Galligan,' said Daniel.

'Same to you, Daniel. Enjoying your holidays?'

'Well, trying to.'

'That's the spirit.'

Daniel sat down. About the same age as David, perhaps a little older, he was much smaller in stature and gave the impression that he was smaller in mind too. Even if he was not, a glance at him with his cousin soon portrayed him a 'yes man' by nature who only played second fiddle to David. However, beneath this veneer of feebleness one sensed maturity that came with suffering, and a readiness to obey reason rather than emotion which was not so apparent in David. If Daniel was vain, his vanity was well camouflaged underneath a nervous manner and had certainly not been allowed to manifest itself in a goatee like David's, even though their tastes in dressing were much the same. Daniel sat quietly for a while and then tried to say something but hesitated.

'What's the matter, Dan?' asked David. 'You're looking worried. Is anything wrong?'

'Yes — I mean, no. Well, er — ' It was obvious that what he had to say was urgent but meant for only David's ears. Father Galligan realized the situation.

'Well, David,' said the priest, rising, 'I think I'd better go and talk to your father in the church after all.'

'Why so suddenly?'

The priest scratched an itching chin reflectively, a glint of mischief in his eyes. Then he said:

'Who was it that said that it was bad enough to interrupt an old man's prayers but much worse to stop two young men discussing their holiday exploits? You know, I've completely forgotten who said it.'

'Don't fool us, Father,' said David, smiling. 'No one said it.'

'Then I just did.' They all laughed and the priest left.

'Cunning old Paddy,' said David as soon as the door shut. 'I like him.'

'Has he gone to make your father change his mind?' asked Daniel, sitting up anxiously.

'No,' David replied despondently. 'He's on his side.'

'What?' Daniel was scared out of his wits. 'In spite of the telegram?'

'Yes, in spite of the tele–' David stopped abruptly and stared at Daniel. 'Hey! How did you know about the telegram?'

'How do you think? I sent it!'

'I might have guessed. Why did you do it?'

'Don't look at me like that! Since it didn't look as though we could dissuade your father, I thought the only man who could would be the priest. Your father obeys him without question.'

'Well, he's only come to reinforce my father's determination. I'm afraid the game's lost, Dan.'

'Oh my God!' Daniel sighed. 'What are we going to do?'

'Ask me another!'

'There's still one last hope, though.'

'What?'

Daniel looked down to avoid David's eyes.

'Well?' David said once more. 'What is it?'

Daniel's voice shook slightly as he spoke. 'We, we, we –' he stammered, evidently choking with fear.

'We what?'

'We could confess, couldn't we?'

'What?' David nearly roared the thatched roof off the house. 'Confess? Have you gone mad?'

'Confession is the one sure thing that could disarm your father now. Don't you think so?'

12

'Are you seriously suggesting,' said David, 'seriously suggesting that you and I walk up to my father and tell him that we are secret members of the Ozo-Ebunu Juju society?'

'Why not?'

'Just like that?'

'Well, he'd be shocked, naturally, but it would produce the desired result.'

'Have you considered the consequences?'

'Excommunication from the Church is not too high a price to pay for your father's life, is it?'

'Damn it all! Who cares a banana about excommunication?'

'Then what consequences do you mean, David?'

'At the university, you fool. Have you forgotten that I'm vice-chairman of the Black Power Society? And that you're a member of the executive committee? Have you forgotten our resolutions, our programmes, our commitments? Standing up at meetings to shout about the vindication of African personality has no meaning at all unless we are prepared to back it up with action. This is our first real test and you want us to flinch.'

'But there's nothing wrong in telling your father that—'

'How can we tell him that we are members of the society without letting out some secrets of the society? It is a matter of priority, Dan. I don't know about you, but I'm not prepared to betray one of the oldest institutions of Africa in order to placate an old fool who happens to have a mania for Roman Catholicism. I'm not going to sell the African personality which I am sworn to uphold. I mean, how can you possibly make this confession without betraying our Black Power Society, thousands of students looking up to us, and our great nation? You want us to turn renegade to the cause that will create a new nation just to please an old man? No, Dan. The fact that he's my father is an accident I'm quite prepared to regret, but can't help.'

'Yes, David, but don't you think that your father feels for his religion what we now feel for our cause? Put yourself in his place.'

13

'It's not the same thing. My dear man, can't you see that, to my father, religion is no longer the worship of a deity. It has become a psychological anchorage.'

'How do you mean?'

'The Africa my father knew in his youth is different from the Africa of today. The love and tranquillity of those early times when society was predominantly what we now call primitive communalism are fast being replaced by competition and change. Finding himself surrounded by chaos, he has to clutch on to something. That's all religion means to him now, a spiritual pillar to which to harness a dispossessed soul blown hither and thither by the winds of change and anti-change. He doesn't see this as a choice between the rational and the irrational but as a life-and-death fight between survival which Christianity epitomizes and destruction which everything anti-Christian promises.'

'But David, if this is so, why punish him for it? Why must we destroy this illusion which he finds life-sustaining? Some people prefer to be happy in self-deceit than to be unhappy in frankness.'

'So, you'll let a masochist set his fingers on fire just because he enjoys pain?'

'Listen to me, David; let's not drag improbable abstractions into this. I know we're committed to negritude, but there's a limit.'

'Poppycock! Name me one country in the world that sets a limit to the expansion of its own indigenous culture. England and her conservatism? Russia and her slavonism? Japan and their kimono and chopsticks? Or is it China and her Cultural Revolution?'

'At least one of them's not quite true, David.'

'In what way?'

'Because, left to the extreme slavonics last century, Russia, for all we know, might still be under Tsarist domination today. It was the pro-Western radicals who imported Marxism from the West to bring about the decisive revolution. Remember?'

14

'Yes, but without the slavonic spirit, that underlying belief in the Russian national and cultural integrity, this would have been impossible. You can see its manifestations everywhere in Russia today. For instance, the writings of Dostoevsky are still tolerated in Russia because of their slavonic flavour.'

'Aren't you making an unbalanced comparison here, David?' Daniel asked. 'The literary gimmick of a dead writer and the terrorist activities of a living organization?'

'Here we go again!' exclaimed David indignantly. 'Laying all the emphasis on the tough aspects of it alone. Quite conveniently, no one mentions the invaluable contributions the Ozo-Ebunu Society has made towards law and order in this part of the world. Rules binding its members, rules against stealing, adultery, murder, rules that beggar the ten commandments of the Church. Rules to maintain social order founded on democratic discipline. No one seems to realize that the Juju society is the oldest source of constitutional law in the land. The commandments of the Church aren't terrorism. Even the promise of hell fire isn't terrorism, not even blackmail. But the disciplinary measures of the Juju circle are terrorism. What makes my gorge rise is that our people still don't know the facts of life where culture and wealth are concerned. When you talk about the preservation of culture, they always think you're talking about national pride while, in actual fact, you're talking hard economics. The highest priced commodity in the world market is neither gold nor diamond, but culture. And it's been that way right from the beginning of human society. The moment a people convinces the rest of humanity that their way of life is best for the rest of the world, their culture, which after all is nothing more than the way they cope with their particular physical environment, becomes automatically a commodity for sale, and, what's more, they fix the price. This is why a little country like England has performed a miracle of empire-building and progress with nothing more than coal for a natural inheritance, why Africa exports her natural wealth to Europe with nothing in return but European culture, and why our people are still dying of poverty

15

and are reduced to a state of cultural scavengery and animality
from which, if we don't take care, they'll never rise again. Isn't it
cute, Danny Boy?'

'And you think that the remedy to these ills is sacrificing
your father tonight?'

'Sometimes, even the most abominable of means are
justified by the end.'

'Even if the end is that of your father and the abominable
means carried out by his own son?'

David looked up and suddenly frowned. 'What d'you mean?'

'Obviously,' Daniel replied with deliberate slowness, 'you've
overlooked the most ruthless of the circle's rules. The one that
makes me tremble right now.'

'Which one?'

'The rule that, when someone's got to be liquidated, his
nearest blood relation in the society is entrusted with the job. Has
it occurred to you, David, that whatever they decide to do to your
father tonight, it is you they'll charge to do it?'

David was silent for a moment and, when he spoke, his
voice sounded husky and subdued. 'You know, I've often
wondered whether a High Court Judge would ever pronounce a
death sentence on his own mother if the circumstances ever arose.'

'David, the circumstances have arisen. And you're not a
judge; you're an executioner. If they ask you to kill your own
father tonight, will you do it? Will you murder him, David, will
you?'

After a long pause David jerked his head up suddenly as if
someone had stuck a needle into the back of his neck and, looking
Daniel straight in the eyes, said grimly:

'We'll cross that bridge when we come to it. You're looking
tired, Dan. There is some brandy in that cupboard behind you.
Perhaps a gulp will do you some good.'

He got up and, without saying another word, left the room.

*   *   *

16

Catechist Thomas arrived at his post of ambush five minutes before midnight. Sitting on an old stump, his gun carefully laid on his lap, he was protected from view by a thick growth of bush overlooking the narrow path from which he expected the approach of the enemy. High above his head, tropical foliage had intertwined to form a splendid canopy in which, here and there, the night sky could be seen. All around him the old man saw huge brown stems arching above the ground many yards from where the parent tree stood. The river sang softly in the distance, while a rabbit gnawing kernels in the hollow of a nearby tree seemed to provide the musical accompaniment.

Suddenly Thomas heard the noise of running feet. He was surprised that it was not coming from the expected direction, but from the bush behind him, along the narrow bush-path by which he had come himself. Whoever it was knew that the old man was there because the sound was coming straight to him. He jumped to his feet in a flash, aimed the gun, and, the next moment, would have fired but, recognizing who it was, he steadied himself.

'Sir, sir,' a voice called out desperately, 'put your gun down. It's me.'

'Daniel!' shouted the exasperated catechist. 'You foolish boy! I might have shot you down. What are you doing here at midnight? And tonight of all nights!'

'Sir, I must talk to you.' Daniel was out of breath and his words came out in jerks.

'What, now? When the Juju will be coming up that road at any moment?'

'That's why you must listen to me. It's urgent.'

'What is it that can't wait till tomorrow morning?'

'If you don't listen to me, sir, there'll be no tomorrow for either you or —' Daniel hesitated.

'Or whom? Speak up, Daniel. We haven't got all night.'

'Sir,' began Daniel haltingly, 'there's something you must know.'

'Well, be quick about it.' The old man glanced towards the

17

road. 'Time's running out.'

'Sir, I think you ought to know that, that —'

'Speak up, boy. This is no time for "that-ing". You hear me?'

'I think you ought to know that, that, em, I mean, yes, well, that —' He suddenly stopped short and yelled out: 'No, I can't tell you! I can't! I —'

'In that case, clear off at once. This is no place for hysterical boys.'

'But, sir,' pleaded Daniel, 'you can't do this to yourself. This thing is more complicated than you think. So complicated I can't even tell you. Please try to understand. You mustn't fire that gun whatever you do. Give it up. Go home now, now, now. Oh, my God!' He covered his face with his hands and began to cry. The catechist watched him silently and, placing his hand on his shoulder, smiled, and began to speak gently.

'Why don't you go home yourself, son? Hah? I know you're worrying about me and I am grateful. But it's no use. If there was the remotest chance of me changing my mind, you know it's not you who would be dissuading me, but my son, David. He cares for me as much as you do but he knows his father's ways better, don't you think? And he has accepted the inevitable. He's at home waiting for me. Now, why don't you too do just —' He stopped abruptly and looked up apprehensively. 'What's that?'

The tom-tom had begun to sound down the hill.

'Oh my God!' exclaimed Daniel. 'The tom-tom!' He leapt to his feet. 'They're here. I must run.'

'Yes. Leave me at once. Fly!'

Daniel ran faster than he had ever done before, panting, trembling, muttering incoherently, till the bushes swallowed him up.

The old man, now alone, jumped to his position, agile and tense, and pointed the gun down the road in the direction of the tom-tom beats. The sound drifted nearer and nearer. And soon, the Iga drums began thumping more fear into the air. Every moment was like an eternity of dreadful suspense. And then, as if

18

from the very archives of the dead, a voice that sounded anything but but human, a voice that focused your imagination on immortality whether you liked it or not, the 'tangible' voice of the Ebunu Juju, began a weird solo. Hearing 'Him' was dreadful enough, but when the towering column that was 'Him' soon appeared as well, the old catechist felt he was under some inexplicable spell; the shivers ran down his spine and he wondered which beat louder, the tom-tom drum or his heart. If you brought here an unbeliever in the Juju divinity, one thing was certain, he would never depart an unbeliever. But Catechist Thomas was not merely an unbeliever. Like doubting Thomas of old, his stubbornness was such that he disbelieved invincibly till he saw the evidence with his own eyes and dug at the wound with his own pointer, in this case a gun.

The Juju was not alone. There must have been at least thirty henchmen with 'Him'. The muscles of their buttocks were tightly girded with loin cloth, the biceps constricted by arm-bands made from leopard skins. Razor-sharp matchets glittered in the moonlight as their holders swayed in tempo with the Iga drumming. At first, the catechist wondered what it was that dangled from their hips, long flat things that reminded him of cowboys wearing gunbelts. He soon realized that these were scabbards from which the knives had been unsheathed. None of the men wore shoes.

'And why should they?' their thumping feet seemed to ask. The soles of their feet were harder than steel and the sun-baked tropical soil was not complaining. Towering above them all like a coconut tree among weeds was Divinity Himself. His weird conical frame was escalating up the hilly road as if pulled along by an invisible crane. The earth trembled with their approach and the crickets stopped singing. The henchmen took over and chanted like warriors on the warpath.

'Ufo ka-ana efo m,
Ufo!
Ufo ka-ana efo m,
Ufo!
Ufo nke ana-efo oka-aka bu ufo ana efo m,

19

Ufo!
Ufo ka-ana efo m,
Ufo!
Ufo nke ana-efo ekpe-nta bu ufo ana efo m,
Ufo!
Ufo ka-ana efo m,
Ufo!
Ufo nke ana-efo mgbala-aku bu ufo ana efo m,
Ufo!'

Catechist Thomas did not move. He watched their approach in silence and waited till they were about twenty yards from his hiding-place. Then he took a deep breath and shouted at the top of his voice:

'That's enough! Stop where you are! Juju and all! You've come far enough!'

The Juju and his henchmen, taken by surprise, stopped immediately and stood where they were. The drumming and chanting also stopped instantly. There followed a momentary silence.

'I want you to listen to me carefully,' said the catechist. 'I want all of you to get off the Mission's property at once. At once, d'you hear me? At once!'

In answer, the Juju resumed his solo as though the old man had not spoken at all. And branching off from the road, He and the henchmen headed towards the catechist's place of hiding. The henchmen began to roar a defiant chant.

'Stop, I tell you,' screamed the catechist. 'I have a gun.' But he was completely ignored. The Juju sang even louder. 'I'm warning you,' shrieked the old Christian, 'I'll shoot you down. Stop!'

It was of no avail. They still ignored his shouts.

'This is your last warning,' he said almost pleadingly. 'Don't push me any more. Please.'

There was still no change in the tempo. The catechist was now dripping with sweat, but he stood his ground.

20

'All right,' he called angrily, 'as a man of God, I'll give you one more chance. I'll count ten. And, if at the count of ten you don't stop, I'll shoot down your Juju. You hear me?'

Then he began to count, slowly at first and even slower towards the end.

'One!

Two!

Three!

Four!

Five!

Six!

Seven!

Eight! — I'm warning you.'

Nine! — I warn you for the last time.

Ten!' And bang! Bang! went the gun. An instantaneous silence followed the reports of the gun. No chanting, no Iga drumming, no tom-tomming. Just an absolute soundlessness. The catechist lowered his gun, a glint of triumph in his eyes.

'He's down,' he whispered as if trying to convince himself. 'The Juju's down! I thought they said he was immortal.' Looking Heavenwards, he made a sign of the cross and heaved a sigh of relief. 'Thanks be to Thee, O God,' he whispered. 'Now that Thy servant has done his humble duty, he must return to Thy House and give Thee Thy due thanks.' And placing the gun on his shoulder, he turned away proudly, and set off up the path.

He reached his house about ten minutes later. As he mounted the doorsteps, his voice was blaring away *Agnus Dei* in unison with the fall of his steps. He was in ecstacy. He did not even wait to get into the house before breaking the good news to his son.

'I'm home, David,' he shouted, 'and triumphant! I told you I'd cripple the Juju, didn't I?' He unlocked the door. 'Well, I have done just th——' To his surprise, the room was in darkness.

'Lord of Mercy! David's gone to bed. He hasn't sat up to wait for me after all. Still, never mind!' Then he walked across the

21

room, a vague figure in the dimness, and put down the gun. He looked around him reflectively. Only a stray moonlight beam enabled him to get his bearings. It was hard to believe that this was the very parlour which had been deluged by sunlight at mid-day. There was also an uncanny sort of silence.

Opening a chest, he took out a box of matches and proceeded to light the Alladin lamp on the table. Meanwhile, he carried on his monologue: 'Still, if our Lord didn't reprimand His disciples too harshly for not keeping vigil with Him at Gethsemane, who am I to reprimand my son for not doing just that in my humble abode?'

Presently the lamp was lit and the old man was able to see that David had not gone to bed after all. He was sitting in the chair, eyes closed, mouth open, head dropped backwards, and the newspaper he was reading when his father left him still lying open on his lap. The catechist gave a start when he first saw him. 'Lord of Mercy!' he said. 'He must have put off the lamp to save oil and then gone to sleep. You did sit up after all. Poor boy, I misjudged you.' Then he called out: 'Wake up, boy, wake up.' But David did not stir. 'David! David!' The old man shook his son by the shoulder and no sooner had he done this than David's body slumped forward on to the floor, lying face upwards. The newspaper now out of the way, two bold patches of blood were clearly visible on his chest. The catechist began to tremble and fell on his knees beside David's body.

'David?' he cried, his eyes wild in their sockets. 'My son? Dead?'

He touched the wounds on his son's body as the original Thomas must have done to Christ's and, raising his blood-smeared fingers to the light, stared at them unbelievingly.

'Two bullet-holes?' he said deliriously. 'Made by my own bullets? But how? But how? But how?'

And just then, as if in answer to his questions, the Iga drums, tom-toms, *enenke* trumpets, elephant tusk-horns, and the chanting of the Juju henchmen began sounding all at once outside his window

22

t had a ring of triumphant mockery about it and that eerie
suddenness which produces a jarringly shattering effect on the
nerves. And then, as if from the very archives of the dead, a voice
that sounded anything but human, a voice that focused your
imagination on immortality whether you liked it or not, the
tangible' voice of the Ebunu Juju, began a weird solo. The
catechist rose slowly to his feet, raised his roving eyes, and
stared unseeingly into space.

'And,' he said huskily, 'and I didn't believe in Divinity!'

All through that night he could not sleep. Early next
morning, he got out of bed, went into the parlour, and knelt
before the huge crucifix, which, at times like this, served him as an
altar. As he mumbled his prayer, the loop of the chaplet swayed
from side to side, one bead after another delayed temporarily
between his fingers in solemn caress. Pale and mournful, the
heartbroken old man was on the verge of tears, and might have
given way had not a gentle knock sounded on the door. He crossed
himself, got up, walked over to the door, and opened it.

'Please, come in, Father,' he said with a broken voice.

Father Galligan, breathing hard from hurrying, was hardly his
usual calm and jovial self. His hair was dishevelled, his features
racked with anxiety and pain.

'I came as soon as I got your message,' said the priest with
great concern. 'This is dreadful news.' He sat down, clutching the
arm of the chair nervously.

'Most, most dreadful, Father,' the catechist sighed and sat
opposite the priest.

'How did it happen?'

'The Almighty Designer in Heaven,' he crossed himself, 'He
alone knows how, Father.' The old man's voice was flat. 'David
was here when I left last night. He was reading the *Herald*. He said
he would wait till I returned. I even made him lock the door from
the inside before I left. But when I came back, the room was in
darkness. As I put on the light, I found him still in the very chair
he sat in when I went. The paper was still in his hands. But he was

23

dead, killed by the very bullets I had fired at the Juju. I don't know what to make of it, Father Galligan.'

'What happened at the place of ambush? Did you carry out my instructions?'

'Word for word, Father. First I ordered them off the Mission's property. Then I warned them I had a gun. Finally, I counted up to ten, exactly as you instructed.'

'Yet they never stopped?'

'Never! Instead, they turned and headed straight for me. I had to shoot in self-defence.'

'Did you actually see the Juju collapse?'

'I thought I did. But I'm not so sure now. Everything was like a nightmare, hazy, horrifying, fiendish.'

'What did you think you saw? Try to remember. It's important.'

'Well, I thought I saw him fall forward on his knees. The henchmen quickly gathered around him. I thought they were going to take the body away and I made my escape.'

Father Galligan slapped his thigh angrily.

'There must be an explanation,' he said.

'Yes,' agreed the catechist, 'but what?'

'Tell me, between the time of the shooting and when you found David's body, did you ever let the gun out of your sight?'

'Never!'

'Was the door still locked when you came back?'

'Certainly. I had to unlock it with my own key. David never left this room last night. Of that I'm certain.'

'Any signs of people breaking into the house?'

'Not one.'

'This is inconceivable.'

'I wonder.'

The priest looked up in astonishment.

'You wonder what?' he asked.

'If it's that inconceivable after all.'

'Have you any idea how it could have happened?'

'I wish I had.'

'Then what do you mean by you wonder if it is inconceivable?'

'Simply that one thing is beginning to be conceivable to me, Father' answered the old man. 'Perhaps the Juju has some quality of divinity after all.'

'What?' shouted Father Galligan in protest.

'What other plausible explanation is there? Let's face it, the shots I fired at the Juju nearly a mile from here came to be embedded in my son's heart right here in this room. And, according to the doctor's report, the time of the shooting and the time of David's death coincided. To top it all, a few moments after I found David dead, the Juju began singing as if nothing had happened. The bullets hadn't so much as scratched him. He must have some divine powers indeed.'

'Stop blaspheming!' Father Galligan said heatedly. 'I won't have my catechist imagining things like a heathen.'

'Perhaps the trouble was that I started too late. I might have saved my son's life.'

'If Abraham was willing to sacrifice his son, Isaac, to demonstrate his faith in God, why can't you, Thomas? Have you forgotten Job and his leprosy? Christ's temptations in the wilderness? The martyrdom of His apostles? Perhaps God didn't want you to destroy just the Juju with bullets. He wants you to annihilate the very conception of it with sheer Christian faith, the kind of faith that enabled little David to annihilate Goliath, the giant, with a sling. A demonstration of faith in God now that your son is dead is the very last thing this Juju lot may expect. The tables must be turned against them. They've hit you on one cheek. You must now knock them off balance by turning the other. This is your great moment, Thomas, the opportunity every true Christian prays for but rarely has, the privilege to demonstrate true faith in the face of tribulation. Think of it, Thomas. You can't succumb now.'

'No, Father,' replied the catechist after a pause. 'I didn't do it for faith. It was pride. I can see it all now.'

25

'Nonsense!'

'Yes, Father. Pride cost me my son. The poor boy practically begged me on his knees not to do it. It was as if he knew it was he who would have to pay the price, not me. And, like a fool, I was too stubborn to listen.' The old man began to sob. 'Lord of Mercy! I murdered him. I murdered my son. I mur—'.

Thunderous knocks on the door interrupted him. And before the startled men had time to answer, the door burst open and Daniel rushed into the room. He looked greatly agitated.

'Daniel!' exclaimed the catechist, taken aback when he saw the young man's face so horror-stricken.

'What's the matter, Daniel?' asked Father Galligan. 'You're shaking like a leaf.'

'I heard you were here, Father Galligan. So, I came to make a confession. It's urgent. Very urgent,' he added, looking imploringly at the priest.

'In that case,' said Catechist Thomas, struggling to his feet, 'I think I had better go and —'

'No, don't go, sir,' said Daniel quickly. 'I think you'd be interested in what I have to say.'

'All right,' said Thomas, resuming his seat.

'Well?' Father Galligan said, raising his eyebrows enquiringly.

Daniel licked his dry lips nervously with an equally dry tongue, the expression on his face betraying an internal conflict of some sort. The wind shrieked angrily outside and a lizard could be heard struggling desperately against it on the thatched roof above. Daniel took a deep breath and, with a disarming unexpectedness, said to his impatient listeners:

'I killed David.'

'What?' roared Catechist Thomas. 'You what?'

'No, sir,' said Daniel speedily, 'don't get me wrong. I don't mean killing in that sense. What I mean is: I could have prevented his death but I didn't. I feel responsible for his death.'

'You mean you actually know how my boy died?'

'Yes, sir.'

'Now, Daniel,' said Father Galligan, 'supposing you sit down and tell us what all this is about. From the beginning.'

'Thank you, Father.' Daniel sat down.

'Well, come on,' urged the catechist.

'Easy, Thomas, easy,' said the priest with a consoling smile. 'Carry on, Daniel.'

Daniel took another deep breath and began his story.

'David and I joined the Ozo-Ebunu society secretly last year.'

'What?' yelled the catechist.

'I thought as much,' murmured the priest. 'Go on, Daniel.'

'We have a rule in the society: whenever they have to deal with an enemy or a traitor, his nearest blood relative in the society is assigned the task of dealing with him. That was what happened yesterday. They knew you were determined to shoot at the Juju, sir. So, your son had to be made to put on the Juju mask. And you shot him.'

'Lord of Mercy!' The catechist groaned. 'Why didn't you tell me, Daniel? Why didn't you? You could have stopped me.'

'Why do you think I came running down the hill?' said Daniel half-crying. 'I tried to tell you then, but I just couldn't. I was afraid. The penalty for betraying the circle is death.'

'I don't understand this,' said Father Galligan. 'David was at home when his father left, wasn't he? And the door was locked.'

'Yes.' Daniel began to explain. 'But he left soon afterwards. It was his orders. The pretence to sit up and read newspapers till his father's return was all part of the plan. The idea was to create the impression that David never left the room that night.'

'But how did his body get here before I returned?' asked the catechist.

'Oh — that was easy,' answered Daniel. 'After he was shot, he was quickly unmasked, put on a stretcher, and rushed home. Remember, when you came back, you went first to the chapel, to give thanks. They used the key in David's pocket to unlock the door. The rest was easy.'

'The clever devils!' said Father Galligan.

Daniel continued:

'Then they hid in the Bougainvillaea bush outside and waited.
When you returned, they gave you a few minutes to discover the
body and then began their victory chant. They even gave me the
voice distorter and made me sing the Juju solos.'

'Why you?'

'Because, with David dead, I was your nearest of kin in the
circle.'

'St. Patrick! This is the most incredible thing I ever heard in
my life!'

'And now, Father Galligan,' said Daniel after a short silence,
'I've made my confession. Will you please give me the last
sacrament now?'

'Last sacrament!' repeated Father Galligan in awe. 'What
are you talking about?'

'I told you,' answered Daniel. 'The penalty for being a
traitor to the circle is death.'

'But none of them knows you have said anything to us.'

'And you don't think', added the priest reassuringly, 'that
now we know what they are capable of doing, we will betray you
to them, do you?'

'That is immaterial, Father,' replied Daniel. 'Whether the
other members of the circle know it or not has nothing to do with
it.'

'What d'you mean?'

'The oath,' Daniel explained. 'No traitor to the circle outlives
his act of treachery by an hour. Don't smile, Father. It's not funny.
You might as well smile at the mention of the law of gravity when
an iroko tree is falling over you. Divinity is omniscient,
omnipresent, omnipotent.'

'Utter balderdash!' exploded the priest. 'You just told us
yourself that the circle is only a secret society of villagers. Even
you have put on the mask. What then is divine about it?'

'Father Galligan,' said Daniel quietly, 'I don't expect you to
understand. You see, Father, it's far easier for a confirmed pagan

28

to understand the Holy Trinity than for a confirmed Christian to appreciate the divinity of our Juju. Thanks to my upbringing, I'm on the borderline between the two. I like to think that I understand them both.'

'Ha! What's there to understand about this thing?'

'I see you're still incredulous, Father Galligan,' continued Daniel, 'and there's not much I can do about it because my time is short. So I'll just say to you what I said to a member of the circle who jeered at the Holy Trinity.'

'And what would that be, Daniel?'

'That it's a mighty universe in which we live. Most of the mysteries are yet unknown. It's only a fool who doesn't appreciate his own insignificance and pretends to know everything. But a wise man doesn't presume to know, he prefers to listen. The youth of Africa today has become like a pendulum, Father, a pendulum oscillating between Europe and Africa through a mish-mash of dissimilar beliefs and contradicting philosophies of life. Ours is an inheritance of dilemma. Our only key to this dilemma is impartial enquiry, not pedantry! Dogmatism is the most virulent enemy to clear-thinking, Father Galligan, whether in Christianity or Juju Mysticism!'

'You're talking blasphemy, Daniel!' said the priest.

'Oh, I'm feeling tired.' Daniel groaned. 'I feel faint.'

'Poor boy!' said the catechist. 'Look, Father Galligan, his eyes are turning white.'

'Do you have some brandy here, Thomas?' asked the priest.

'Yes, over there. On the table behind you.'

'Splendid!' Father Galligan poured some brandy into the glass and handed it to Daniel. 'Drink it down, boy. It'll revive you presently and make those superstitious ingredients evaporate from that crowded head of yours.'

'Thank you, Father.' Daniel sounded hoarse.

'Hold your hand steady, Daniel,' said the priest. 'What's the matter with you?'

The glass was only half way to Daniel's lips when,

suddenly, the drums and tom-toms started thumping down in the village. The glass fell from his hand and crashed in pieces on the floor, soaking the mat with brandy. He began to sway as if in a daze.

'Hey! Father! hey!' cried Catechist Thomas frenziedly from where he was corking the brandy bottle. 'Catch him. He's falling off the chair.'

But Father Galligan never made it. Daniel had crashed to the floor and lay among the glass debris, quite still. The little pool of brandy on the floor soon began to take refuge in his white shirt like spilt red ink on blotting paper. A spectacle case slid from his breast pocket on to the ground. Outside, the tropical wind hissed like an upset widow, the hiss of someone not unused to hissing. The cloud gathered in the sky and, in the distance, the thunder rippled away, far far away on the other side of Umunuko hills. A butterfly escaping the wind flew past the window but was soon trapped in a spider's web spanning the angle between the wall and the thatch extension. Father Galligan stooped down and examined Daniel's motionless body. After a while, he rose, an expression of horror disfiguring his face.

'Why are you looking like that, Father Galligan?'

'Good God, Thomas!' whispered the priest disbelievingly, 'It can't be! It just can't be!'

'What is it, Father?'

'He's dead,' said the priest. 'Daniel's dead.'

'Daniel? Dead? He too, dead?' The catechist reacted like a mad man. He fell on his knees, grabbed Daniel's prostrate body by the neck, and began to shake it violently.

'Daniel! Daniel! Daniel!' he shrieked at the top of his voice. Daniel's mouth jerked open like a toy's, his face contorted with the agony of death. Catechist Thomas, frightened and confused, flung the corpse back on to the floor.

'You're right,' he said, backing away slowly. 'Yes, you're right, Father Galligan. He's dead.'

The priest nodded, at a loss for words.

30

'And he was right, too,' said the catechist grimly.

'Who?'

'Daniel. He must be right.'

'What about?'

'He hasn't lived an hour since breaking his oath.'

'Rubbish! Sheer superstition!'

'Is it?'

'My dear fellow, fear can kill a man!'

'Then examine his chest.'

'What has his chest got to do with it?'

'A black circle always appears on the chest of the Juju's victim. David told me. And there was one on David.'

'All right, Thomas! If it'll make you feel any better, I'll unbutton his shirt and we'll have a look.'

But when the priest disclosed Daniel's chest, he was horror-horror-stricken by what he saw.

'There *is* a black circle on his chest.'

Outside the wind groaned mournfully. The clouds were dispersing rapidly as the sun, in a mad rush, seemed to be chasing an invisible soul towards an overhead position in the sky. Perhaps, after all, the gates of Divinity's Hell were situated right overhead. Catechist Thomas, now peering meekly through a window, wondered why most things in life often began as an answer without a a question and usually end up a question without an answer. He sighed helplessly and was about to turn away from the window when those drums and tom-toms began pulsing once more. And then, as if from the archives of the dead, a voice that sounded anything but human, a voice that focused your imagination on immortality whether you liked it or not, the 'tangible' voice of the Ebunu Juju, began a weird solo.

THE SCARECROW OF NAIROBI

It was a stormy night. Thunder and lightning can be frightening anywhere in the world. But in the Kiambu districts of Kenya, it is always a staggering experience. The clap seems to lash out its fury on doors and windows all at once while the lightning threatens to saw you in half with a sword of fire. Tonight's storm was one of the worst ever, and the white farmers had every reason to worry. But the middle-aged couple in the Garden Estates, just off Thika Road, had more than one reason to worry. A Kiambu Mission clock was chiming half past the hour in the distance.

'Albert,' called Mrs Gibson from the bedroom. But Albert did not answer.

'Albert, dear,' she called again. There was another pause. 'Albert, aren't you in the sitting room?'

'Now what!' muttered her husband under his breath.

'I heard that, Albert. What's eating you tonight?'

'I'm sorry, darling.'

'I s'ppose you've had another trying day on the farm?'

'Yes, dear. And some of the things I'm reading in the papers aren't exactly cheering.'

'And you have to take it out on your dear wife, I suppose? An old family tradition!'

'I said I'm sorry, Mary.'

'It's all right,' she said, chuckling. 'I was only joking.'

'What did you want, anyway?'

'Oh, what was I going to say? — yes, your revolver! I was looking for your revolver, dear.'

'My revolver? Whatever for?'

'For under your pillow, dear. I'm getting the bed ready.'

'And so?'

'Surely, Albert, you haven't forgotten what you said to me only this morning.'

'What in particular?'

'That from tonight onwards, you want your gun under your pillow, or within reach in bed.'

'Oh, I see. Don't worry about it, dear. I've got the revolver here with me. I'll fetch it along when I come to bed.'

'What d'you mean: when you come to bed? Aren't you coming yet?'

'Not yet, Mary. I want to sit up till Susan comes home.'

'Oh no!' said Mrs Gibson. She came into the parlour and sat facing her husband. In a dressing gown she was very attractive for a woman in her late forties, dark seductive eyes, freckled chin, long loose hair that fell about her shoulders, her tiny pink toes showing through semi-circular openings on the top of her slippers. The expression on her face was only too familiar to her husband. He knew what was coming and folded the newspapers. 'Stop worrying, Albert,' she began. 'The way you talk, anyone might think Susan had gone to the other side of Mars. She's only gone to the Stanley Hotel, dear.'

'Yes, Mary,' said Albert Gibson sternly, 'but it's well gone eleven-thirty, you know.'

'The show only finished at ten-thirty,' she countered.

'That was nearly two hours ago, Mary.'

'These teen-age shows don't always finish on time, you know. Especially when it's the Beatles. They've been dreaming about the Beatles' tour of Africa for ages. And, at last, their dream's come true. I can just imagine them now, shrieking for more and more encores. Would you believe it! The Beatles in Nairobi!'

'Are you kidding?' said Albert. 'I spend fortunes every year trying to keep beetles off my crops.'

His wife chuckled. 'Come off it, Albert,' she said. 'You know very well what I mean.'

'How's she coming back, anyway?'

34

'Who? The beetle?' She burst into laughter.

'This is no laughing matter, Mary,' her husband replied, and then repeated with great concern: 'How's Susan coming back?'

'As she went off, of course,' his wife answered, 'in the same car as the Salters' kids. They'll drop her at the bottom of the road, just after Muthaiga Police Station, because they are driving into the Kiambu township. Then Susan will just walk up the road, and she's home sweet ho—'

'What!' burst out Mr Gibson. 'Is she walking up the Thika road on her own? Alone? In this terrible storm?'

'What's wrong with that? She has her raincoat, hasn't she?'

'Do you realize how far it is, Mary? Nearly five miles! And on the other side of Kimathi Common too!'

'So what?'

'You astonish me, Mary. An eleven-year-old white girl walking the streets of Kiambu at this time of the night! And you sit there cosily asking me: so what!'

'But Albert — ' his wife was about to protest.

'Yes, I know,' he interrupted. 'I know, I know, don't remind me, I know. This is a tough country, and we've decided to bring up our Susan to be a tough, self-reliant, able woman. Like your parents brought you up. But this is too much, Mary. Times have changed.'

'But Albert, our Susan isn't the only white girl who has gone to this show. If all the other white parents carried on the way you do, all Nairobi would be roaring like an Algerian revolt.'

'And isn't it? How many white families have left already? And if those staying behind only took enough trouble to read these papers, they'd worry all right, don't you worry.'

Mrs Gibson knew that her husband's temper was rising and tried to change the subject.

'What's in the papers then?' she asked with a willing pupil's smile.

'Here!' Mr Gibson struck the newspapers with the back of his huge hand. 'You can see it on practically every page.'

'See what, dear?'

'Black racialism, that's what! It's like a plague, Mary. They call themselves the Land Freedom Fighters. With their bows, arrows, spears, pangas, home-made zip guns, and what-have-you, they are pledged to drive the last white farmers from the country. They think that the land of milk and honey promised them before the magic Uhuru has not yet materialized because of the white man's presence in the country. These hot-headed Kukes on noisy motor-bikes are screaming for an all-black Africa. They won't be content till the last white man's driven out. They're becoming increasingly vociferous, Mary. And dangerous!'

'But surely, Albert, the responsible politicians do realize that without the white farmers the country's economy will collapse. You said so yourself. It takes time to raise cash crops. Three years for coffee. Seven for sisal. Most of the African farmers have neither the experience nor the capital.'

'Yes, Mary, dear, but it's not the responsible politicians that I'm worried about. It's the nine million land-hungry Africans they have to cope with that constitute the real problem here. The masses are like the sea. And the leaders, responsible or irresponsible, are just like fishes. Without the water, the fishes just won't exist. That's why leaders always have to compromise with the appetite of the people they lead. It's happening right now in this country. What d'you think the resettlement schemes are for? I can't see any future for the sixty-thousand whites here. I really don't. We're going to be squeezed out in the end. This is the nemesis of democracy. It sacrifices quality to quantity.'

'This doesn't sound like you, Albert. You've always said that we would stick it out, come what may. We were born here, we belong here, and we're staying here.'

'Yes, I know I've said all that, Mary, love,' replied Mr Gibson, rubbing his rough chin meditatively. 'I've babbled my own share of the good old clichés. It was part of growing up, I s'ppose. But we have to face reality in the end. As a young man, I dreamed dreams. And now, as an older man, I'm seeing visions which don't

36

quite click with my dreams.'

'I don't understand.'

'It's true we were born here, Mary dear. But we've never belonged here really. And probably never will. A horse born in a mule stable does not automatically become a mule.'

'Nonsense!'

'No, Mary. We've not really lived in Africa, if you know what I mean.'

'No, I don't.'

'We merely grew up in these little segments of Europe carved out here and there on the continent of Africa. Like living in little oases in a desert. But now they're going to destroy these oases and expose us to the scorching realities of desert life.'

'And you dread the adjustment? You, Albert the Lionheart, my own brave Albert, are afraid?'

'Let's just say, I'm not looking forward to it.'

'Meaning that black and white can't live together?'

'I'm a farmer, Mary. Not a sociologist. But I know one thing for certain. If these newspapers are anything to go by, it'll take a rough period of adjustment, believe me. Only this morning, an African reader wrote a letter to the editor. And d'you know what he says?'

'What?'

'He suggests that the best way to demonstrate that the country has thrown off the European imperialist shackles, as he calls it, would be to change the traffic lights to national colours of red, green, and black. I mean, if black nationalism is assuming such racialist dimensions, can you quite frankly see the black and white people blowing kisses to each other in our lifetime?'

'Quite frankly, Albert, I see nothing racialist in this man's suggestion. Stupid nationalism perhaps, but definitely not fascist.'

Mr Gibson threw the papers on the floor in anger. 'You know,' he said, 'sometimes I wonder whose side you are on.'

'I thought you knew, Albert,' said his wife, grinning, 'I'm on the side of the colour-blind. There're only two types of people I

37

hate: the jews and the gentiles. Come on, Albert, smile. Don't be so damned miserable about nothing.'

'I don't know how you can take these things so lightly.'

'Simple. My imagination's not half as lively as yours. Besides, you worry enough for both of us.' She laughed. Just then the doorbell rang. 'Ah —' she said, 'that must be Susan. It's all right, dear,' she said to her husband, 'I'll let her in. Silly girl, she's left her key behind again.'

'Thank goodness she's safe. Now I can breathe normally again.'

Mrs Gibson was out of the room only a few moments before she came back, wearing a bewildered expression.

'Albert,' she whispered, 'it's not Susan.'

'No?' Albert showed a little concern. 'Then who is it?'

'A man. An African.'

'What?' Mr Gibson sat up. 'At this time of night? Is it one of our shamba boys?'

'No.'

'What does he want?'

'He wouldn't tell me. He says he wants to speak to the master of the house.'

'That's odd. What sort of man is he?'

'Oh, seems all right to me. You know, well groomed, cultured voice, quite polite — you know, the intellectual sort. And quite handsome too —'

'You can spare me the details, woman. I merely asked you to tell me what sort of African he is, not to undress him.'

'Albert!'

'Never mind! Don't let him hear us arguing. I'll go and see what he wants.'

When he got to the door, he saw a huge ebony-black man with a balding head and a thick black moustache. The man must have been about forty, and his clothes, a Ghana-styled kente jumper and long linen trousers, were wet with rain. His eyes were bloodshot and he spoke with a Paul Robeson bass.

38

'I'm sorry to trouble you at this time of night, but something eadful has happened.'

'What is it?' asked Mr Gibson as his wife joined them.

'There's a body lying down the road,' said the stranger.

'What?' said Mrs Gibson, seizing the man by his shoulders. 'What? Where? I mean, what kind of body?'

'A woman, I think. I didn't get close enough to see. I didn't ant to touch anything. I came straight for help.'

'God, what have I done!' cried Mrs Gibson. 'Albert, do you ppose it's – ? Oh – my God! Susan!'

'My raincoat, Mary,' ordered Mr Gibson. 'Quick!'

'Yes, Albert. I'm coming too.'

The storm was still raging when they got to the common. ey had run all the way but none of them had time to think of edness.

'There she is,' cried the strange African. 'There, on the grass.'

'Yes,' cried Mrs Gibson, 'I can see her, Albert. Oh! This is vful.'

'Don't come any closer, darling,' said her husband. 'I'd tter go and see first.'

'But Albert –' she was about to protest.

'Damn it,' Mr Gibson exploded. 'I should have known better an to let you come along.'

'He's right, madam,' said the strange African. 'It might be a sty shock for you.'

'All right, all right,' replied Mrs Gibson heatedly. 'I'll wait re then. You men go and find out.'

'Come on, you.' Mr Gibson did not like the idea of this rican acting in advisory capacity to his wife, even with the best intentions. 'Hurry, man, hop it.'

'Stop giving me orders,' retorted the African sharply. 'Are u blind? Can't you see I'm right behind you? I'm not your useboy, you know.'

'Okay, you two!' said Mrs Gibson. 'Don't make a revolution t of it. Get on with it.'

39

By then the two men had arrived at the spot where the body lay. Mr Gibson turned the body over.

'Tell me quickly, Albert,' said Mrs Gibson impatiently. 'Is it? — is it? —'

'No, Mary, thank goodness. It's not our Susan.'

Mrs Gibson sighed with relief and, remembering that whoever it was was somebody's 'our' somebody, she exclaimed quickly: 'Oh, but who is it?'

'It's terrible, Mary,' replied her husband. 'A nun!'

'Look!' the strange African shouted, pointing at the body on the wet ground. 'She's alive.'

'You're right,' agreed Mr Gibson. 'She's breathing. Yes — she's really coming round now.'

The nun began to groan.

'Yes, Albert,' cried Mrs Gibson joyously, 'I can hear her. Oh — thank God. Can I come near now?'

'Yes, Mary, I suppose so. She seems to be —'

Just then, the nun began to scream hysterically: 'Take your hands off me! Let me go! Let me go!'

'Take it easy, now,' said Mr Gibson, trying to console and help her up. 'Take it easy. You are all right now.'

'Don't touch me!' she screamed even louder. 'Go away from me.'

'Poor thing,' said Mrs Gibson. 'She's in quite a state, isn't she? I think she'd had a terrible fright.'

The nun saw her for the first time.

'Oh, we're not alone,' she said with relief.

'Of course we're not alone,' said Mr Gibson. 'You're perfectly safe with us. My wife and I have come to help you.'

'And,' added Mrs Gibson quickly, 'and this gentleman, of course. It was he who discovered you in the first place.'

'He?' asked the nun in astonishment. 'Then it wasn't he who, who, who attacked me? Aren't you a police officer then, Mr —'

'Gibson's the name. Albert Gibson. No, I'm not a police officer. I'm a farmer. We live just along the road.'

'Then what happened?' asked the nun.

'I was just going to ask you the same question. We merely found you lying here.'

'But I thought you said you came to my rescue. You mean you let him get away?'

'Let who get away? There was no one here when we arrived. Can you stand on your feet now?'

'Yes, I think so.'

'Here,' said the strange African. 'I'll give you a hand.' He offered her his massive shiny black arm. The nun looked at him undecidedly.

'Oh, I'm so nervous,' she said.

'Come on, take my arm, too,' said Mr Gibson, and they helped her up. 'Now, sister, would you care to tell us what happened?'

'Oh my Lord!' cried the nun. 'I'm doomed, finished, ruined. Why didn't he just kill me? You arrived too late. Much too late.'

'What happened, Sister?' asked the strange African.

'It was a man,' the nun explained. 'A strange man. Oh my Lord!' she exclaimed suddenly.'It was awful, awful! I'm no longer . . .'

'What?' shouted Mr Gibson. 'You don't mean, you, you, you don't mean he did this to you right here on the common?'

The nun nodded and began to cry.

'What was he? African?'

'Well,' replied the nun, 'I, I think so.'

'Can you describe him?'

'No more questions, Albert,' interjected Mrs Gibson. 'You're not making things any easier for her.'

'Yes, you're right, Mary. You'd better stay here with her.' And changing his mind, 'On second thoughts, no. Under the circumstances, I'll stay here with them while you go for the police, Mary. And hurry!'

41

'No, no, no,' the nun protested at once. 'You mustn't. Don't go for the police, whatever you do. Please, I beg you.'

'But why the devil not —' began Mr Gibson furiously, but soon checked himself, 'I mean, why not?'

'The shame would kill me. It really will —'

'Nonsense. The law —'

'Besides,' continued the nun, 'I can't take such a step on my own initiative. I must speak to the Mother Superior first.'

'At the convent, you mean?'

'Yes. I must. Only she can make such decisions.'

'Well,' Mrs Gibson joined in, 'if that's the situation, Albert, I suppose we just have to abide by it, haven't we?'

'In that case,' said her husband, as he helped the nun along, 'you must come home with us now. You've had a terrible shock, and you're cold. You've been lying in the storm too long.'

'No, I don't think I should,' replied the nun reluctantly. 'I've been enough trouble to you already.'

'Nonsense, dear,' said Mrs Gibson. 'It's no trouble at all. Isn't that so, Albert?'

'Certainly. And you don't imagine, young lady, that you can go home by yourself after this, do you?'

'I don't suppose so,' said the nun.

'Then it's settled,' Mr Gibson said with an air of finality. 'After a short rest and a shot of brandy, I'll drive you back to your convent. How's that?'

'You're very kind,' said the nun gratefully.

'Well,' said the strange African, 'from the way things have turned out, I think this is where I wish you all a goodnight.'

'Not on your life,' came Mr Gibson's sharp reply. 'I intend to get to the bottom of all this before I let you out of my sight.'

Mrs Gibson chuckled nervously. 'What my husband means is that you must come home for a drink too,' she explained in a conciliatory manner. 'You know, bottoms up! sort of thing. Ha! ha!'

Ten minutes later they were all sipping drinks in the

Gibsons' sitting room.

'More brandy for you?' Mr Gibson asked the nun.

'No thank you very much. I'm all right now.'

'You're sure?'

'Quite sure, Mr Gibson, thank you. I don't really drink, you know. The little I had was purely as medicine. Because of the shock. And I feel fine now, really.'

'Splendid.'

'Are you new to Nairobi, Sister?' said the strange African.

'Yes,' the nun blushed as she answered. 'And stop calling me "Sister". I'm not even a nun. Another six months to go yet. At the moment I'm only a novice.'

'In that case,' the strange African joked, 'may I call you just — Novice?' He burst into laughter. The nun also began to laugh. 'Excellent,' he said. 'It's good to see you laugh.'

'Personally,' Mr Gibson said strongly, 'I consider the joke's ill-timed.'

'Albert!' his wife called, looking at him reproachfully.

'Tell me,' he continued, eyeing the African with undisguised suspicion, 'tell me, how did you know she was new to Nairobi?'

'Oh —', the strange African scratched his head and studied the nun concentratedly as he explained. 'It's easy to see. She's young and very fair, no tan yet. I bet that, if she takes off her veils, we'll find she is platinum blonde.'

The nun was blushing more and more and the look on Mr Gibson's face was growing murderous. Mrs Gibson, as usual, came to the rescue.

'Hey!' she said playfully. 'Are you a writer or something?'

'Sort of,' replied the African, smiling imperturbably.

'Before we get side-tracked into biographies,' Mr Gibson interrupted, 'I must say you're a very observant young man.'

'I am, you know,' replied the strange African.

'And you're sure you have not observed this young lady somewhere before?'

'Before what?'

'Before tonight's incident.'

'No.'

'Or during?'

'What exactly do you mean by that?' Temper was getting short on both sides.

'Um, er,' Mrs Gibson chirped in, 'do you want some more drink?'

'No, thank you, Mrs Gibson,' replied the African.

'Albert?'

'Mary,' Mr Gibson exploded, 'I would to Heaven you'd stop being so blasted diplomatic. We must bring this thing into the open. I can smell a rat somewhere.'

'You must forgive my husband, you two. Like all farmers, he has a passion for getting at the root of things.'

'No, Mrs Gibson,' said the nun. 'Perhaps your husband is right. I owe you an explanation. You must all be wondering what I was doing alone on the common at that time of night.'

'No, that wasn't what I meant,' Mr Gibson hastened to explain. 'I meant him to —'

'I know,' the nun cut in, 'but I want to get it off my chest.'

'Well,' said Mrs Gibson, 'what happened, dear?'

The nun began her story.

'I was going back to my convent at Kadete.'

'On the other side of Nairobi? Ten miles, I think! You came all that way?' Mr Gibson asked.

'Yes,' replied the nun. 'You see, I'm attached to a little maternity hospital on a Kikuyu Reserve this side. About five miles beyond your Garden Estate.'

'I see.'

'I do what we call the early night duty. Usually, I finish at 11 o'clock.'

'At night?'

'Yes. And then drive all the way back from the unit to the convent.'

'How long have you been doing this?' Mr Gibson was asking

44

all the questions.

'About a fortnight now.'

'So, it would be easy for anyone who has been watching you all that time to predict your movements precisely?'

'Well, yes, I suppose so.'

'I see. Carry on.'

'Well, just as I was driving home tonight, the two front tyres of my car blew up.'

'What, both of them?'

'Yes, Mr Gibson. Why?'

'Hm —' he was thinking aloud. 'I imagine the idea of blowing both tyres was to make doubly sure in case you carried a spare. Carry on, Miss.'

'I was completely helpless,' began the nun but was soon short-circuited again by her inquisitive host.

'I'm sorry to keep interrupting you, Miss, but I want to get the complete picture in my mind. Tell me, where did this — this accident — occur?'

'About half a mile from here. So, I got out of the car and began to walk. I hoped to get help at the Muthaiga Police Station. The rain was pelting down like bullets. And the lightning was unbelievable. I'd only walked about ten yards when I heard something move behind me. I suspected I was being followed. I looked back and was right. It seemed that whoever it was had been waiting for me behind one of the bushes. I walked faster and he walked faster. When I slowed down, he did the same. I looked back again and could see, even through the rain, that he was a wild sort of a man — and huge! He swayed from side to side like a scarecrow.'

'A scarecrow!' exclaimed Mrs Gibson. 'How terrifying!'

'He must have been drunk,' the nun continued, 'a tramp of some sort. He carried a long stick and I was afraid that, if he overtook me, he was going to knock me down with it and, and, well, and then take what he was after. From time to time, he sort of jerked his hand to his mouth. Like a mad man. Only a mad person would try to smoke a cigarette in that tornado. There wasn't a single soul in sight besides the two of us. I had this dreadful feeling that something terrible was about to happen. Oh, it was awful! I was trembling all over, more from fear than cold. It was like being in a haunted house all alone and trying to escape when you see all sorts of phantoms around you and the doors locked. I became aware of a peculiar sense of powerlessness which I could do nothing about. Powerless in the hands of a sex-maniac. I increased my pace. But it was no use. His single pace was equal to six of mine. I trotted forward. But because I kept looking back, I didn't notice when I reached a dip in the ground. I stumbled, fell into a pool of water. I heard the man make a funny sound in his throat. Perhaps he was coughing, but I wasn't sure. Most probably he was laughing at me. In fact I think he stood still for a while. I made another effort, struggled to my feet, and began to walk, but he followed me again. I walked as fast as I could, but he kept gaining on me. I remembered what I'd read in the papers before I left England and particularly what an African friend was telling me while shopping in Nairobi only this morning. You could have heard my heart beating miles away. At last, I began to run. We were now in the middle of the common. This was when it happened. I ran into an old tree-stump, fell down, and must have fainted. I've a weak heart, you see.'

'And then?' asked Mr Gibson.

'Can't you guess? Do I have to say it?'

'No! Not that!'

'The next thing I remember was you leaning over me.'

'Are you sure he interfered with you while you were unconscious?'

'Why else would he have been chasing me? Nothing's been taken from me. Nothing material, that is.' She began to sob.

'I understand this may be a little embarrassing for you, dear,' said Mrs Gibson, 'but tell me, how do you feel? Bodily, I mean.'

'I'm not sure,' the nun replied. 'Certainly not normal. Damp and sort of messy all over.'

46

'Yes, dear, but don't forget you fell into a pool of water.'

'True, Mary,' said her husband, 'but she's also covered with cigarette ash. Or do you smoke, Miss?'

The nun shook her head.

'Don't you think you ought to be seeing a doctor,' asked the African, 'to make sure.'

'I'm sure the Mother Superior will see to that.'

When the nun had finished her recital, she was taken to the bathroom by Mrs Gibson to tidy up before Mr Gibson drove her home.

'Now that the two women have left us together, Mr Kalenjin,' began the white farmer with startling bluntness, 'I'll speak to you quite frankly, Black Leopard.'

The strange African raised his eyebrows only slightly, still as unperturbed as ever.

'I recognized you the moment you walked in through this door,' Mr Gibson went on.

'Yes?'

'And besides knowing that you're the editor of the new chauvinist paper, *Black Uhuru,* I also know that you're the brain behind the extreme group that call themselves the Black Power Liberation Front.'

'Yes?'

'Yes, Mr Kalenjin, I do have my means of knowing these things.'

'Do you now, Mr Gibson?'

'Yes. Espionage is essentially a European art, you know.'

'Then you must have found out enough to realize that learning is essentially an African art. We're good learners, Mr Gibson. So much so that we very often surpass our teachers. I too have mastered your means of knowing things – as you call it. I too recognised you, the moment you came to the door. I know that, besides being Mr Albert Alphonso Gibson, the rich benevolent white farmer, you're one of the leaders of the new anti-black wing of the white underground movement.'

'At least,' said Mr Gibson, 'our movement is there for a

noble cause. The protection of the whites and minority interests from your malicious intentions.'

'Yes, I get your message.' Mr Kalenjin had thrown off his pretence of timid amiability. 'The protection of the whites is a noble cause but the protection of the blacks is a malicious one. Is that it?'

'Protecting the blacks! Ha! Is that what you call it? Was that what you were doing tonight? Ha? Attacking a defenceless young girl, a convent novice. Do you call that defending the blacks?'

'What are you insinuating, Mr Gibson?'

'Come on, Kalenjin, own up to it, man. Can't you see it's all too obvious? You organized this whole thing, didn't you? You know as well as I do it was one of your boys that attacked this girls.'

'Who's kidding who?' replied Mr Kalenjin. 'You know very well that whoever assaulted that girl is on your pay-roll. This is a premeditated plan by your white Klan to blemish the reputation of Africans before world opinion. And this isn't the first time you've done it, either. Presenting us as thugs, cattle-stealers, and rapers of religious virgins. Well, you've miscalculated this time because I'm taking this matter to Mzee personally. And through him to the United Nations. And I don't have to tell you to watch out for the headlines of my paper tomorrow morning. You'll see.'

'What the hell!' began Mr Gibson but he was interrupted by his wife who ran into the room shouting:

'Albert! Albert! Albert!'

'What is it, Mary?'

'Albert, it's Susan.'

'What about Susan?'

'She still isn't back.'

'What? I thought you said – '

'Yes, I said she might have come back and gone to bed while we were out. But she isn't there, Albert. I just looked into her room.'

48

'Good grief! Ring the Salters at once.'

'That's what I'm telling you, Albert. I just telephoned them. Their children got home long ago. They dropped Susan just down the road and said she ought to have been home over an hour ago.'

'Mary, something terrible's happened. I knew it all the time. I could feel it.'

'Wait a minute,' said Mr Kalenjin suddenly. 'Did you say your daughter's name is Susan?'

'Yes, why?'

'Yes,' said Mr Kalenjin reflectively, 'I think that was what he called her.'

'Who called who Susan?' Mrs Gibson was on the point of tears. 'What are you saying?'

'How old's your daughter, Mrs Gibson?'

'Eleven.'

'And she wears pigtails?'

'Yes. But —'

'And glasses?'

'Yes. But where —'

'Black raincoat and a white hat?'

'Yes. That's Susan all right. Did you see her?'

'Yes. She was with a man when I saw her.'

'What man?'

'I don't know.'

'Well, what sort of man?'

'Now that I think of it,' replied Mr Kalenjin slowly, 'it could be that same man who attacked the young lady down on the common. The description fits him perfectly.'

'How long ago was it you saw them together?'

'About five minutes before I found the lady's body.'

'Which way were they heading?'

'Towards the valley, I think. You know, in the opposite direction.'

'But why didn't you rescue her? Why didn't you call the police or something?'

49

'There seemed no need to.' Mr Kalenjin shrugged his shoulders. 'They seemed friendly enough. They were even holding hands.'

'Holding hands!' Mrs Gibson cried. 'Oh my God!' In desperation she turned to her husband. 'Albert, he's got our Susan; that sex-maniac. What'll we do?'

Mr Gibson rose to his feet and confronted the African.

'All right, Kalenjin,' he said. 'We've played this game long enough, don't you think? How much d'you want?'

'How much do I want for what?'

'I want my daughter back,' Mr Gibson roared. 'Susan is all we have. She's all our life. I'll give you anything you want. Anything. And I promise you I won't go to the police. We'll even leave the country tomorrow if you wish. All I ask is my daughter's safe return. Please.'

Mr Kalenjin burst out laughing.

'I must congratulate you on your performance, Mr Gibson,' he said. 'It's almost convincing.' And then shouted angrily: 'You cunning swine. The Beatles show, the nun's attack practically in your front garden, the kidnapping of your daughter by an African who takes great pains to be seen holding hands with her! What a marvellous coincidence, Mr Gibson! It shows to what ridiculous lengths a man of your calibre would go to paint Africa black, even though you won't keep it black. Imagine paying a man to kidnap your own daughter. You dirty crook!'

At this Albert Gibson landed him a blow on the chin. Kalenjin struck back. Mrs Gibson pleaded with them to stop fighting, but in vain. The nun, hearing the noise of crashing bodies, rushed back into the room. She joined with Mrs Gibson in trying to separate the two men but only succeeded in being knocked down herself.

Suddenly there came a loud rap at the door.

'Sh-sh-sh. Can you hear that?' said Mrs Gibson. The fighting stopped at once. 'Someone's at the door.'

'Did you telephone the police, Mary?' asked Mr Gibson.

50

'No. But perhaps they've found out something about Susan.'

'Then open the door and find out.'

But when Mrs Gibson opened the door, she cried out:

'Susan! It's Susan!'

In came a little fair girl with sharp darting eyes, eyes as blue as a Siamese cat's. Her dress was exactly as Mr Kalenjin had described, her hat and coat dripping water all over the floor. She had a habit of opening her eyes wide when she spoke.

'Hello, mummy. Hello, daddy. I'm sorry I forgot my key again.'

'Don't worry about the key, darling,' said her father. 'Are you all right?'

'Of course, daddy. Why? And what was all that noise I heard just now? Were you playing a game or something? And daddy! Your ear is bleeding.'

'Never mind that, my girl. You just tell us where you've been tonight.'

'Oh,' exclaimed Susan, turning away from her father, and faced the nun, 'there you are!'

'Me?' asked the nun.

'Yes, you,' Susan replied. 'Are you all right now?'

'Have you seen me before?'

'Of course. It was you on the common, wasn't it?'

'You saw me lying there?'

'Yes, I saw you fall. I saw everything.'

She looked about her worriedly. 'Why are you all looking so shocked, daddy?'

'Did you,' her father began, 'Susan, did you say you saw what happened?'

'Yes, daddy.'

'The whole thing?'

'Yes. Why?'

Mrs Gibson collapsed on to the chair. 'Oh no!' she gasped. 'Albert, tell me I'm dreaming. Tell me it's not true.'

'This is all your doing, Mary,' her husband raged. 'I told you

51

not to let her go. The Beatles' show is great, you said. And see what you've done. You've exposed her to more great shows than one. Now, what are we going to do?'

'Come over here, Susan,' Mrs Gibson called. 'Come and tell mummy what you saw.'

'Over my dead body!' protested her husband. 'You're not going to make an innocent girl re-live such a horrible experience all over again. Not in her imagination, even. Who can tell what psychological effects this is going to have on her!'

'But, Albert, that's precisely why I want to get it off her mind now. The least we can do now is help her understand the horrible and animal nature of the whole thing before it's too late.'

'Your wife's right, Mr Gibson,' said the nun, only just recovering from the blow she received in the fight. 'Only that way can any abnormal psychological effects be dispelled.'

'All right then,' agreed Mr Gibson. 'Come here, Susan.'

The bewildered Susan approached her father.

'Now, listen to me, darling,' Mr Gibson pursued. 'You said you saw what happened between this lady and a man on the common tonight.'

'Yes, daddy.'

'Now, tell us about it, darling. Everything.'

'Yes, daddy. I got out of the car down the hill.'

'Yes.'

'And started walking home. Then I saw this nun running out of the common as if someone was chasing her. I looked and really saw a man following her. All of a sudden, she fell down. I was frightened and hoped she would get up before the African reached her — I remembered what you told me about people like that.'

'Good girl! And then?'

'She didn't get up. She just lay there. Then the man came nearer, and nearer, and nearer —'

'And what then, Susan?'

'A surprising thing happened.'

52

'What surprising thing, Susan?'

'I told you I thought she was running away from him.'

'Yes?'

'But when he got where she lay, he just walked past her.'

'What?' all exclaimed at once.

'Yes,' Susan confirmed. 'He just walked on.'

'You mean he never even stopped?' asked Mrs Gibson.

'No.'

'He never even touched her?'

'Why should he touch her, daddy?'

'Well,' said Mr Gibson, obviously at a loss what to say, 'well, what I mean is, Susan, his manners, didn't he try to help her get up? I mean, a gentleman must always help a lady in distress.'

'But this man couldn't, daddy. He didn't even know anyone was lying there.'

'How do you know, Susan?'

'Because, daddy,' Susan went on, 'he was blind.'

'Blind!' repeated Mr Gibson, confused.

'Yes, daddy, he was just a blind man in need of help. So I helped him across the common and then came back to help the nun. I tried to lift her up but she was too heavy for me. I could only roll her over to the other side, and some cigarette stubs stuck all over her. I brushed some of them off with my hanky. Then I was about to come home and tell you about her when I saw the blind old man still groping about. Because of the storm, he'd completely lost his sense of direction. So I asked him to let me take him home. At first he objected, saying that my parents might get worried about me. But when I told him what a wonderful understanding mummy and daddy I have, he agreed and gave me his address. And I took him home. It seemed such a shame to leave him groping there like Rhody. Remember Rhody, daddy? The blind old rabbit you gave me once, the one killed by a cat because he couldn't get away?'

'A blind man!' whispered the nun in self-reproach. 'Of course, why else would he have staggered like that? And I thought

53

he was drunk! How stupid of me not to see it right away from the colour of his stick! Poor blind African! Poor, poor old man. It was he who was in need of help.'

'For the first time in my life,' said Mrs Gibson, 'I'm glad to hear that a man is blind.'

'Poor, poor, blind, helpless man!' the nun continued. 'I was a pig! Oh, my Lord! What have I done! It's like crucifying you all over again.'

'No, Miss,' said Mrs Gibson, holding the nun's arms like a consoling mother. 'It's not your fault. It's all those sensational stories in the papers. It's all very well and amusing to a reader who's far away, but a very different thing to those on the spot. See the complication it has created, making you read a nightmare into the harmless movements of a blind old man.'

Little Susan, still bewildered, wondered what the fuss was all about.

'Did I do wrong, daddy?' she asked.

'Of course not, darling,' said her father, stroking her head. 'Whatever put that idea into your beautiful little head?'

'But you and mummy looked ever so worried because I said I had seen the whole thing.'

'No, darling. You're beginning to imagine things. You know what that means, don't you?'

'What, daddy?'

'That you're in love.'

'With whom, daddy?'

'The Beatles, of course. Who else?' He laughed.

'Oh — daddy,' exclaimed Susan, 'you're right. I do love them. I love them. I love them. Oooooh —'

'You did enjoy the show then?' asked her mother.

'Oooooh! It was smashing, mummy. Thanks for letting me go. Thanks, daddy. Oh, they're so fab, so —'

'All right, Sue,' said the mother, laughing. 'Tell us all about it tomorrow. Off to bed now.'

'All right, mummy. Goodnight, mummy. Goodnight, daddy.

Goodnight, everybody. And daddy —' she called from the door suddenly.

'Can I bring Beulah to my birthday party next Saturday? She's going to telephone me tomorrow to know what you say.'

'Who's Beulah?'

'Beulah of course,' said Susan, surprised at her father's blatant ignorance. 'She's the blind African's daughter. She's not even blind, daddy. She's super and she's only one month younger than me. She wants me to come to her birthday party, too. Next month. Can she come on Saturday, daddy? Please! Let her come.'

'Of course she can. Can't she, Mary?'

'Yes, absolute must!'

'And,' said Mr Gibson, 'when she rings tomorrow, tell her she can bring her father along.'

'Can she really?' Susan was beside herself with excitement.

'I insist upon it,' replied Mr Gibson.

'Oh, daddy, you're the most gorgeous father in the world. And you're the most gorgeous mummy.'

'Thank you,' said Mrs Gibson, laughing. 'Goodnight, dear.'

THE MEDICS

To think that one of the most incredible experiences of my life
began and ended in one hour! I had decided to leave the Ugwuoye
Hospital at precisely a quarter to one. The sun was at its peak
above the horizon and the sky tinged orange with the sun's rays.
As I walked out of the hospital gates, I heard the tyres of a vehicle
shriek to a halt behind me. It was a little convertible Opel car
with a rather disturbing dent engulfing the right headlamp. Another
inch forward and the bonnet might have knocked me down.

'Isn't that swell!' exploded the driver, his accent
unmistakably American. I mumbled a few words of apology and,
stepping out of his way, hurried on. The car started off again,
whisked past me, and, to my surprise, made another brisk stop a
few yards in front. Thrusting his head out of the window, the
driver peered at me through thick sunglasses as I came nearer.

'Pardon me,' he said, 'but aren't you Obi?'

'Yes,' I stopped.

'The writer?'

'Yes.'

'Just come home on a nine-week holiday from England?'

'Yes.'

'Well, don't look so flustered, man,' he said, beginning to
laugh. 'Newspapers do get to us sometimes, you know. Even in
this God-forsaken place.'

I felt that the last remark was calculated to test my patriotic
sensitivity. The sly expectant smile on his face confirmed this.
So, instead of volunteering a direct response, I made a drawl in
my throat, one of those funny guttural sounds one often acquires
in England and finds so handy under such circumstances for the
simple fact that they are uninterpretable. My American friend
wiped the smile off his face.

'Visiting a patient, were you?' he asked. 'Or just looking around?'

'Looking around is more like it,' I answered. 'Just seeing what progress the hospital has made since I left home.'

'And were you impressed?'

I made another throaty noise. He frowned.

'Can I give you a lift somewhere?'

'It depends on where you're going.'

'No, it depends on where you're going,' he said decisively. As it happened, I was only walking down the main road to catch the one o'clock bus for Onitsha. I told him so.

'Really? I'm driving to Onitsha myself,' he said. 'To get our week-end supply of sausages from the Kingsway. Well, what are you waiting for? Hop in, man, hop right in!'

I thanked him, got into the car, sat beside him.

'Oh, by the way,' he said as we drove off, 'you're not in a mad hurry, are you?'

'Not particularly,' I answered.

'That's okay, then.'

'Why do you ask?'

'I've one little call to make on the way, that's all. Just an assignment. Won't take long. You don't mind, do you?'

For some reason, the picture that came to my mind was that of some lady teacher's hideout somewhere in the far-away village where my American (probably lady-killer) friend was going to spend a delectable half-hour. I thought of all sorts of things that could happen there, possible introductions, maybe I would be asked to sign a few autographs and then get an invitation for a second visit. It had been my experience in the past that every other lady expects a writer to be somewhat inclined to Bohemianism and would go to great lengths to patronize it if it is truly there, or invent it if it is not. The affair always ended up the same way: in anything but marriage!

'No,' I answered my American friend, unable to hide my tickled anticipation, 'I don't mind at all. Take your time. Don't rush your — assignment.'

We turned left into the main road and began to tear through Egbema village like a meteor. I didn't even notice when we passed Nnubia's Residence on the left, not to mention Ilona's and Unegbe's. Obviously, my friend enjoyed his driving and was in love with speed. He pressed a button and the roof of the car folded up like the leaf of a sensitive plant. He was full of youthful zest, not more than twenty-five, blonde, and lanky. He wore a white short-sleeved cotton shirt, no tie, and a pair of light bible-black shorts. His white jacket, bearing a Harvard University athletic badge on the pocket, lay on the back seat of the car. He stepped on the accelerator, looked at me, and smiled.

'Do you enjoy writing?' he asked suddenly.

I didn't want to ruin my friend's driving with another guttural noise.

'Sometimes,' I said. I anticipated his next question. Usually, it was at this point that people say to me: 'You know, I've never met a writer before now,' to which I would reply: 'Now you have; you can see we have three hands.' This always provoked a giggle and made me feel I had passed a wit test. I had repeated this very reply more times than I cared to remember and, each time, as I said it, I tried to make it sound spontaneous as if it was the very first time the question was ever put to me and my first time in answering it. I gave my American friend precisely ten seconds to spit out the stereotyped question. You can imagine how shattered I was when, in less than five seconds, he asked:

'What d'you write about?'

'I beg your pardon?'

'I said: what d'you write about?'

I was floored, completely at a loss what to say. But, suddenly, I remembered a passage in Alexei Peshkov's book where a character was saying under similar circumstances:

I think you will agree with me if I say that the purpose of literature is to help man to know himself, to fortify his beliefs in himself and support his striving after the truth; to discover the the good in people and root out what is ignoble; to kindle shame,

wrath, courage in their hearts; to help them to acquire a
strength dedicated to lofty purposes and sanctify their lives
with the holy spirit of beauty. This, then, is my definition;
clearly it is sketchy and incomplete; you may add to it
whatever else serves to refine life, but tell me, do you
accept it?

I had read this passage many many years ago, long before the
dream of writing ever entered my head. In my schooldays,
words had for me the same charm and beauty that well-arranged
flowers hold for women. I made love to words by memorizing
them, repeating passages I liked over and over again till my
whole being became soaked in their magic and wisdom. It is
amazing really how anything memorized in childhood days is
wrapped away like fossil in your mental bedrock, while the
memories of later years often evaporate like Eau-de-Cologne on a
lady's temple. '*Nauta:* sailor, *agricola:* farmer, *aqua:* water, *terra:*
land, *amat:* loves.' I could still recite from the first page to the
last, and exactly as arranged in the textbook, all the Latin
vocabulary I learnt in my first year in the Grammar School; but
if you were to ask me the motto of the hospital I just visited, I
couldn't tell you without consulting my notebook even though I
had taken time to study it. At the moment, however, my problem
was neither Latin grammar nor the motto of the Ugwuoye
Hospital. My American friend was waiting for his answer. What did
I write about? If I answered him: novels, plays, poems, or whatever
else I liked to think I wrote, it would have a Jack-of-all-trades, not
to say pompous sort of ring. Besides, it wouldn't be a witty
answer. And besides, how was I to know he wouldn't follow up
with: what kind of novels, what kind of plays – since all I would
have told him really was what I wrote, not what I wrote about!
No, this won't do, I thought. My immediate impulse was to recite
verbatim Peshkov's passage on the purpose of literature, beginning
with 'I think you will agree with me if I say that the purpose of
literature is . . .,' and ending with 'do you accept it?' On second
thoughts, I decided against this. Supposing he knew the passage

60

too! What if he had read it! I had met quite a few American young men in my time and while, on the whole, I had found cause to question the depth and originality of their thought, I had never doubted the broadness of their reading. Paradoxical when you think of it! What would this boy think of me, I said to myself, if he stopped me in the middle of my recital and said with that sly smile of his: 'Sorry to interrupt you, fellah, but you left out a word,' and then completed the paragraph for me. He looked the kind of chap who would do just this kind of thing and talk about it later with gusto! This was more than a little disturbing. And, even if he hadn't seen this passage in all his life and I succeeded in getting away with reciting it, his question would still be unanswered. He had not asked for the purpose of literature. His question was what I wrote about. I scratched my knee thoughtfully. To my amazement, I heard my voice say:

'Oh, I write about humanity and its problems.' I stopped there. I could have enlarged upon this, but thought it best not to. There was nothing like a laconic answer in a situation like this. It gave one a philosophical aura, creating the impression that you knew much but said little.

'Humanity and its problems, h'm?' said my friend, half asking, half snorting.

'Yes,' I said with the same laconic air, ramming down the philosophic impression with another guttural eruption.

'Then I'm mighty glad you're coming with me,' said my friend.

'Coming where with you?'

'To this assignment I told you about. You know, the place we're gonna call at before we start going to Onitsha. I thought you didn't mind.'

'Yes, I know. But you just said you are glad I'm coming. Why?'

'Because it should interest you, if you write about human problems. I know you're born in this part and all that, but now that you've tasted Western civilization and had the benefit of its

61

education, I'm sure you'll see your African way of life very differently from the way you did before leaving home. Perhaps a glimpse into the sort of problem we have to cope with over here right now will give you something to write about.'

'A glimpse into a problem?' I asked. 'What kind of problem?'

'You'll see,' he said smugly. 'Which reminds me! I haven't told you who I am, have I?'

'No,' I replied.

'Well, I won't keep you in the dark any longer. My name's Dick Gooderick. Everybody calls me Dicky.'

'Hello Dicky,' I said, looking away deliberately to discourage him from offering to shake my hand at the speed we were going.

Five minutes later, we were at Ezenwelike, an inland village noted for its birds and its bosoms. We saw evidence of both and slowed down. This was our destination. Dicky knew the name of the man he wanted, but not his house. We made a few enquiries and, at last, were guided to a large compound surrounded by a thick mud wall which was in turn capped all round with fresh *igbogili.* In the centre stood a mud house roofed with corrugated iron sheets. It looked an ordinary sort of house, nothing outstanding or exceptional. Yet it was in this insignificant compound, a patch of tableland that resounded with the croak of frogs in the rainy season and the cries of infants undergoing circumcision in the dry wakes of the year, it was here that one of the most remarkable characters in the whole continent of Africa reigned like a monarch. This man was Okwologu.

As we came through the front gate, he was in front of the house chopping a log of wood with an axe almost as large as the log itself. He was the most handsome figure of a man I had ever seen. He was not very tall or broad, but there was something about the beard on his face and the muscles of his body that struck you as superhuman. The structure of his chest was like rock, so hard and impenetrable that not a single hair could sprout. Every part of his body sweated profusely except that chest of his. He wore only tight brown tarpaulin pants which, because of the *gworo*-brown

62

colour of his skin, produced an impression of total nakedness till you looked again. His feet were bare and looked so strong and iron-like that you wondered if they wouldn't be more effective on the log than the axe he was using. His head was clean-shaven and shone like the peak of a mountain and through the cascade of hair on the rest of his face, one could make out two blood-red eyes, the bridge of a strikingly wide nose, and a movement of one layer of hair over another that indicated the position of his mouth.

He stopped chopping firewood when he saw he had visitors, put the axe down, and glared at us anxiously.

'Is your name Okwologu?' asked Dicky Gooderick.

'Aha,' the bearded man answered and spat on the ground, 'I am Okwologu Ahuoku, the one and only son of Ikwuamaehi.' My fear of acting as an interpreter was dispelled at once. The man spoke English. 'Have you heard of me, then?' he asked.

'Yes, Dr Williams sent me to you.'

'Aha, aha, aha,' Okwologu replied jubilantly. 'Dr Williams sent you, eh? Any friend of Dr Williams is a friend of mine. Come and sit down please. Anywhere you like.' There were a few *agada* stools which, I presumed, our host was drying in the sun.

'You know Dr Williams, then?' asked Dicky as we sat down.

'Yes. Didn't he tell you? We've been close friends for years. He is one of the few white men who really understand us. And very witty, too. You know what he once said to me? He said that women are expensive whichever way you look at it. They cost more time than money if you're handsome and more money than time if you're not. The old bastard must be bankrupt.' He roared with laughter, his beard parted with his lips, displaying two rows of beautiful white teeth that gleamed like pearls. We joined in the laughter too, more from fear than anything else.

'I was just gonna say,' said Dicky Gooderick, still laughing, 'I was just gonna say that, coming from Dr Williams, a statement like that sounds like self-consolation. Isn't he ugly! A real knockout! And those English-made shirts of his with collars like the ears of an antelope don't do him any good, either.'

Our host frowned. Either he did not care to hear his friends disparaged or he detested youth speaking disrespectfully of age.

'I thought you said Dr Williams was your friend?' he asked.

'Of course he is. He sent me here, didn't he? Why?'

'Never mind! I'll go now and get you some kola.'

'What?' asked Dicky.

'Kola nuts.'

I explained to my American friend that, in Africa, it is the custom to offer visitors kola nuts as a gesture of welcome.

'Yes, I remember reading that somewhere,' he replied.

'I hear that in England you offer tea instead,' our host rejoined. 'Hot tea because the weather is cold.'

'I am not English. I'm American.'

'Yes? If you'll excuse me one moment, I'll go and fetch the kola.'

'No, please don't bother,' said the American. 'I'm not really hungry.'

Okwologu shrugged his shoulders and sat down again.

'You're new here, aren't you, son?' he asked.

'Yes,' replied Dicky Gooderick and, not being quite sure whether the refusal of kola nuts was offensive to African thinking or not, tried to say something complimentary. 'Your English is very good, Mr Okwologu. Where did you learn?'

'Oh, that,' replied our host, smiling. 'I lived with European missionaries at Ihiala for many years when I was a little boy.'

'How come you never became a Christian?'

'My father made me come home when I came of age. To take up the family calling.'

'The family calling?'

'Didn't Dr Williams tell you? My father was a native doctor, the greatest of his time. The power of medicine has been in my family as far back as anyone can remember. It passes from father to son. And must continue as long as life lasts. I was the only son of my father, and he was getting old. We always marry late in our family. Marriage is such an inconvenience to a medicine man. A woman in the house pollutes it. The spirits won't come near and every communication with the dead is by remote control. Terrible for business, marriage is. So we keep it as late as possible, just to have one son to take over from the father when the old man dies. That was how my father inherited spiritual powers from his father and me from mine.'

'Is that what you do?' asked Dicky in amusement. 'You're a witch doctor?'

'I'm a doctor,' replied our host emphatically.

'Then why aren't you made up? Where are your feathers, your indigoes, your goatskin?'

'I'm not a masquerade dancer, son! I'm a doctor. Every white man that visits me here makes the same mistake, always confusing the two. They expect me to put on all kinds of things. I don't know where they get that idea from. A real powerful doctor wears nothing weird. Look at Anaehe Ntaogu of Amakwa, Chukwunwe of Umumpama, Nwakeze of Umuanyioha, Olimmuo and Mbaanughu, or Mmuokwe of Uhuaguma Obiofia.'

'How do you operate then?'

'Take a look at that,' said our host, pointing proudly at a bottle of dark brown liquid standing on a stool. Dicky surveyed the bottle for a while and shrugged in bewilderment.

'I take it you concocted that stuff?' he said.

'Yes, I prepared it myself,' Okwologu replied.

'What for?' asked the American sarcastically. 'For an epilectic hippopotamus, or something?'

'I see. Like all newcomers to this part of the world, you enjoy being brutal with your tongue. I shouldn't if I were you, son.'

'No? Why not? Maybe you're gonna destroy me with some kind of black magic spell or something?'

'No, I wouldn't do that.' Okwologu chuckled. 'Not to a friend of Dr Williams.'

'I don't believe you could do anything.'

'What's your name, son?'

65

'My name is Gooderick, Dicky Gooderick.'

'And what is your business here, Mr Gooderick?'

'Back home I'm a medical student, but, at the moment, I am over here on what we call a Peace Corps mission. I'll be here for about six months, helping Dr Williams. And also advising the natives.'

'Studying medicine, eh?' said Okwologu with a benign smile. 'That's good. We belong to the same profession. Perhaps, one day, you'll be as good as me.'

'Not quite,' Dicky replied steadily. 'You don't understand. I'm studying to be a proper doctor, but you're what we call a witch doctor.'

'What's the difference between the two?'

'For one thing, I'm receiving a proper, up-to-date medical training at a university. But you had no such training.'

'And because of this you believe you've more power than I have?'

'Well, yes.'

'Can you prove your power?'

'Do you doubt it?'

'A little.' He picked up the bottle from the stool. 'You see this medicine, yes?'

'Yes,' replied the American. 'What about it?'

'This medicine can cure yellow fever in five minutes. Can you make such a medicine?'

'Let me see.' Dicky took the bottle from the native doctor, removed the cork, inhaled the content, and shut his eyes in disgust. 'I don't think there's any mystery about this stuff. Pieces of the bark of some tree soaked in alcohol. The bark probably contains some chemical which kills yellow fever germs, to put it simply. And this chemical dissolves in alcohol, which is why you've soaked the bark in alcohol. This reaction is faster at high temperatures which explains why you're warming it in the sun. What's so difficult about that? I bet you can't explain the reaction so technically yourself. What are you smiling at?'

66

'You, son.' Okwologu scratched his beard roguishly.

'Me?' asked Dicky, a little irritated.

'Yes, you. You're so young! What a pity you weren't here nine days ago. You would have seen something that would have made your eyes pop out. And maybe teach you some sense.'

'What happened nine days ago?'

'A fantastic duel. You should have seen it! For the last five years, two young native doctors — as young as you, believe it or not — had been boasting of their medicine skills, each claiming to be more powerful than the other. And the funny thing is that they're the best of friends. One was reputed to have killed his own mother just to use her clavicle in stirring a magic spew and the other had castrated himself and offered his testicles to Udoekwulu vultures in exchange for spiritual powers. Well, nine days ago, these two brilliant devils staged their long-talked-about combat. It was beautiful. And as for the crowds, even the Oye market-place couldn't hold more. It was a great display, believe me.'

'What did they do?'

'All sorts of staggering feats. But the highlight of the combat came when one of them borrowed an egg from someone in the audience and, with this, cracked an entire basketful of hard dry palm nuts, picking up one at a time, balancing it on a stone, and striking the hard shell of the nut with the egg. Instead of the egg breaking, the hard shell of the nut flew to pieces, releasing the kernel inside. For nearly an hour, he sat there doing this, the crowd cheering at every drop of a kernel. When the basket was empty, he invited a little girl in the audience to give the egg a gentle tap with her little finger. And when she did this, the egg broke open like any other ordinary chicken's egg, the liquid stuff inside gushing out like oil from a broken bottle. The crowd rose to their feet and cheered him to the echo, but when he stepped forward to take a winner's bow, the other combatant ran forward like a madman, pulled his loincloth to one side, lashed out his headquarters — if you know what I mean — and began to urinate on the stem of a nearby Ogilisi plant. The tree burst into flames

67

and burnt to ashes while everybody watched. Wonderful, wasn't it?'

'Were you there when this was happening?' Dicky asked. 'Or did someone tell you this and you swallowed it?'

'I was there. I saw it with my own eyes.'

'If you're as great as you said you were, why didn't you compete with them?'

'Don't insult me, son. These were little boys to me. I was their umpire. And to referee at such a duel, the rule states you must be great enough to sit on a blazing log of firewood all through the match.'

'And you did that?'

'Ask anyone.'

'I don't believe it,' said Dicky.

'Please yourself, son.'

'How about doing it again? I bet you five pounds.'

'Why? To convince you that I, Okwologu Ahuoku, the one and only son of Ikwuamaehi, am a great doctor? No, son, betting is for young people and boasting is for half-wits. Great practitioners perform unannounced.'

'You're backing out now, aren't you, great doctor?'

'Laugh if you like, son. You won't be the first Professor Ology to come to Africa. Nor will you be the last.'

'Professor what?' asked Dicky in astonishment.

'Ology,' repeated Okwologu with his roguish smile. 'You mean you haven't even heard the story of good old Professor Ology?'

'No, I haven't.'

'No wonder.' The native doctor had a way of cackling like an old hen when he chuckled. 'Then I'll tell you, son. Perhaps that'd teach you a lesson.'

'You don't say! Then educate me, Doc.' Dicky was enjoying being sarcastic.

Okwologu tugged at his beard thoughtfully and began his story:

Professor Ology was the first white man ever to set foot on

ur soil. His real name was Dr Jackson, but you'll soon see why e's remembered as Professor Ology. When he arrived here, there veren't many roads and bridges, so he asked a young African boy o take him across the river in a canoe. Halfway over, he asked if he boy knew any marine biology. The boy said he knew nothing f the kind. The white man exploded into laughter and said that, vithout this knowledge, the boy was hardly alive. 'By Jove!' he ried. 'One-fifth of your life is gone.' Then he said to the boy: since you don't know any biology, do you know any geology?' he boy said no. 'By Jove!!' the white man exclaimed, laughing, two-fifths of your life are gone. Then perhaps you've read some nthropology?' The boy shook his head. The doctor laughed so udly that people on the other side of the shore wondered what as the matter. 'By Jove!' he screamed, holding his sides. 'Three-fths of your life are gone, you know that? Surely,' he continued, ince you've not spent all your life idling, surely you've read me elementary anthropology? How's your anthropology, my oy?' The boy replied that he hadn't heard the word. The white an, unable to hold himself any longer, threw himself at the ottom of the boat, rocking with laughter. 'By Jove!' he cried nce more, 'Four-fifths of your life are gone.' He laughed and ughed till his shirt was torn and all the monkeys fled into the ngle. His helmet fell off his head and hit the side of the boat. he boat rocked and capsized. The poor African boy, well aware at only one-fifth of his life was now left, swam desperately ashore safety. He turned round, and to his amazement saw the white an still struggling in the river and crying for him to help. The hite professor couldn't swim and was drowning! Then the African outh shouted from the shore: 'Tell me, Professor, do you know y swimology?' The white man cried helplessly, 'No, I don't.' Jo?' cried the young man, 'then, ALL your life is gone.' And, mping and laughing, he ran home to tell his story.

None of us could resist laughing when Okwologu completed s story.

'That's a good one,' said Dick Gooderick. 'I've heard lots of colonial jokes, but I must admit that's one of the best. And I'm glad you brought it up because I want to make one thing quite clear.'

'What's that?' asked Okwologu.

'As long as I'm concerned in this village, the last thing I'll tolerate is any kind of superstition or witch-doctoring. I've travelled all the way from the States to fight these things and that's precisely what I'm gonna do. Do I make myself clear?'

'You want to stop witch-doctoring, do you?'

'You heard me right.'

'Do you know that long before the white man ventured into this village, this witch-doctoring, as you call it, was a highly advanced form of medicine already?'

'That's exactly the trouble. So high and advanced, in fact, that in this twentieth century it has rocketed your infant mortality to a world record.'

'D'you know that before you were born, I, Okwologu Ahuoku, the one and only son of Ikwuamaehi, could cure madness? Do you know that, son?'

'Yes,' replied Dicky sarcastically. 'With a spell, I suppose, that guarantees a cure in five minutes, like your yellow fever stuff Look here, Daddyo, you can fool your people, not me. I happen to be a medical student. Do you know what that means? A medical scientist in the making.'

'Do you know that long before your people invented the telephone, we had our method of sending long-distance messages. With the tom-tom.'

'Your trouble is that you listen to too many political speeches. What you don't know is that your freedom-fighting nationalists make the fiery speeches you echo just for one purpose. To gain power. After they get it, it's us, the people they once decried as robbers, it's us they appeal to for help. I volunteered to come here and help you people because your government sent for me. And while I'm here on this mission, I intend to make a thorough job of it.'

70

'Have you asked Dr Williams's opinion yet?'

'What the hell does it matter what his opinion is?'

'A lot, son. After all, he's got years of experience to back it up. And he's British. The British have been here a lot longer than our people. And they know us better.'

'That's the trouble. Dr Williams has been away from civilization so long he's becoming even more superstitious than you lot. Would you believe it! Thirty years in Africa! He's so out of date it's always a giggle working with him. I wouldn't let him infect me with his stethoscope if I had the misfortune to be a patient of his. If you ask me, it's about time someone organized a special Peace Corps Mission for these European oldies in Africa.'

'Then you did ask Dr Williams?' asked Okwologu, still wearing his mysterious amused expression.

'I did mention my plans to him, yes.'

'And what did he advise?'

'Oh, to hell with it all!'

'What did he say? There's no use getting angry about it.'

'That he disapproved of radical reforms! So what? What you expect from a senile old fellow who, by modern standards, professionally dead? Moribund! That's what irks him. One of the symptoms of age is blind antipathy to reforms.'

'Just as the symptom of youth is blind antipathy to experience.'

'Oh — what's the use!'

'So, Dr Williams advised you not to rush things. Yet you're determined to do just that.'

'Look, man,' said Dicky patiently, 'it's not a question of me being determined. It's a matter of you changing with the times. I don't expect you to understand. But I'm sure posterity will. That's why you must let your son —'

'My son?' Okwologu interrupted, his eyes flashing like a torch.

'Yes,' replied Dicky. 'That's why Dr Williams sent me to come and talk to you.'

'Dr Williams sent you to come and talk to me about my son?'

'Yes. You've got a son, haven't you?'

'Yes, yes, yes. I've got a son. Of course I have.'

'Why do you keep smiling like that all the time?'

'Forgive me, it's a bad habit of mine. What about my son?'

'We've got several reports at the hospital concerning your son.'

'What reports?'

'The first is that your son's got a very serious tongue infection. Is that true?'

'Correct.'

'Is it also true that you refuse to send him to the clinic for treatment?'

'True.'

'Are you afraid of hospitals, Mr Okwologu?'

'Not mister, son. Doctor Okwologu.'

'Oh, what the hell does it matter? Doctor Okwologu, then, tell me, are you afraid of hospitals?'

'Not exactly.'

'Are you sure?'

'It is true I don't want my son to come to your hospital ever. But not because I'm afraid. Fear's something unknown in this family. So don't you start insulting me, sonny.'

'Then why won't you let your sick boy come to the hospital?'

'Because I don't like your hospital, that's why. I'm a doctor. I prefer to treat my son myself.'

'With what?'

'With that medicine in the bottle over there.'

'I thought you said it was for yellow fever.'

'It is also for tongue fever. It's for everything.'

'Isn't that swell!' Dicky was between tears and laughter.

'You don't believe me, son, do you?'

'I believe you believe it, believe me. But how do you expect me to believe it?'

'Do you believe that in your country there's a book that

72

contains the answer to everything?'

'If you mean the Encyclopaedia, yes.'

'Then why d'you doubt that there can be a medicine that contains the cure for everything?'

'Because, because, it's impossible. My ancestors tried it in the middle ages. They called it Elixir.'

'Did they succeed?'

'Shall we say they gave up the attempt when they knew better.'

'You mean they gave up trying when they knew no more?'

'Have you succeeded then?'

'How can you ask such a silly question when the evidence is here before your very eyes? Pick up the bottle and taste just a little.'

'You must be joking. The smell alone has singed the hair in my nostrils.'

'Please yourself, son.'

'Has it cured your son's tongue, yet?'

'Not completely. But it will. I'm sure he'll be able to start talking again in three days.'

'It's also reported that your son doesn't go to school,' said Dicky, looking the native doctor in the eye.

'If by school,' Okwologu replied flippantly, 'you mean your school, the report's true.'

'How old's your son?'

'Fourteen.'

'And you've kept a boy of fourteen at home?'

'Why not?'

Dicky sniffed in disgust.

'Where's your son now?' he asked.

Okwologu looked at the sky thoughtfully.

'You don't even know where your sick son is,' said Dicky. 'You must be a very good father indeed.'

'But I know where he's gone,' Okwologu said as if he had just remembered.

'Where?'

'To the stream. To fetch water. The Eze is not far. I expect him back any time now.'

'Good,' replied Dicky. 'I hope you don't mind if I stay till he returns.'

'Please yourself.'

'Thank you very much.'

'But I must warn you. If your plan is to talk him into going to your hospital and your schools, you're wasting your time.'

'Why d'you say that?'

'He made up his own mind a long time ago. And when he makes up his mind, he's like a rock. You can't move him.'

'And what does he want to do?'

'To take up the family profession. To be a doctor.'

'A witch doctor?'

'Call it what you like, that's what he wants to do. And, as his father, it's my duty to impart this power and knowledge to him. Only recently, he went through his second initiation rite. A point of no return, you understand? The next full moon, he will be spending one night on his grandmother's grave in the cemetery. He wants to be a doctor, our kind of doctor, the doctors who kept people alive in this village long before the white doctors came. It's my son's decision, not mine. And the spirit of our forefathers and the forefathers before them are with him. At the moment, he can make rain, eat fire, turn into a butterfly. He hates your hospitals as much as he hates your schools.'

'We shall see,' Dicky replied. 'Just let me handle him when he returns, ha? And don't interfere.'

'All right.' Okwologu's mysterious smile returned. 'You've said it, my friend. We shall see.'

'Meanwhile I'd like to talk to you seriously.'

'I'm listening.'

'Doctor Okwologu,' Dicky began, 'I want you to know that I understand just how you feel. If I were in your position, I'd probably do the same. You were here long before real doctors

74

came from Europe. And since they arrived, business has been bad for you. The hospitals have attracted away almost all your old clients. You can't compete with scientifically equipped modern hospitals. And your people don't fall for witchcraft mumbo-jumbo any more. Naturally, you've become a little jealous. Frustration has embittered you. I know all this, believe me. And I hate to see anyone, white or black, lose his means of livelihood. But this time, it's got to be done. Surely if you love your people, and I've no doubt you do, you must be willing to make a little sacrifice to further their progress. Let's face it, man, you and I know you're a fraud. The time has come for you to pack it up. We have a saying back home: when you've gotta go, you gotta go. Why don't you just retire gracefully? With those muscles, you could become the richest farmer in this village before you knew it. Be a credit to your people, not a danger.'

'Danger?' The native doctor looked insulted.

'Of course you're a danger,' continued Dicky. 'Take your son, for instance. If his tongue infection is what we think it is, he's in grave danger. If he's not admitted into the hospital at once, he'll lose his tongue.'

'That's a lie,' retorted Okwologu. 'He'll talk in three days.'

'In three days that boy will never talk again. D'you understand? Never!'

'You sound like God himself.'

'And, what's more, the infection's contagious. By keeping him here and letting him go down to the stream, you not only endanger your son's life, but your own as well. And the lives of many other innocent people. We don't want an epidemic on our hands.'

'I knew you weren't worried about my son,' said the native doctor. 'You're worried about an epidemic, the amount of work you might have on your hands, anything but my son.'

'Prevention is better than cure, isn't it?'

'Stop worrying about that. There's nothing here for you to prevent. I told you my son's a doctor trainee himself. He's practising on his tongue.'

'Don't be so naive, Okwologu. If your son wants to be a doctor, give him an opportunity to realize his ambition the proper way. Send him to school. There are thousands of scholarships for boys like him nowadays. You never know, he could go to study in England or –'

'Go to England? My son to England? For what? Go there and spend the best years of his life passing your examinations on your ways of life and know nothing about his own? Maybe he'll come back home with a white woman who can't even stay solid in the sun? Huh?'

'You're mad.'

'Maybe, but before you start asking me to come to your hospital to cure my madness, look around you, young man. You'll see stretches of green land everywhere. If you put down your foot anywhere and raise it up again, you'll find that the footprint you've made contains hundreds of blades of grass. Each blade smells different, heals different, thinks different, even makes love different. Every one speaks to me in a different dialect. And I understand them all. I know their powers and their weaknesses. They all obey my will. This is my kingdom, son. The bark of every tree in this village is to me like the breast of a woman I love. It contains sunshine and the milk of life. I've dedicated all my life to the art of grass mysticism, the art of my father and the fathers before him. My son must learn to give expression to this heritage. If I let him go to England, they'll poison his mind over there. When he comes back home, do you know what he'll do? He's going to clear the bush, cut down the trees and their magic barks, burn these grasses which have been our source of power for centuries. Destroy his kingdom! No, my American friend. My son stays where he belongs: here. What power he cannot get from the spirits, the ghosts, the gods of mystery and guidance, he cannot get in England, I tell you.'

'You really believe that, don't you?'

'Don't you believe in your way of life in America? Your

76

trouble is you do believe in the wisdoms of the land of your upbringing but you deny others the right to believe in their own. I don't blame you though. We've an old proverb which says: no man admits that his mother's cooking is horrible. But you go too far, son.'

'So, this is what you drum into the plastic mentality of a child. How can you do this to your own son? Denying him the opportunities you never had! And the poor boy –'

'Sh-sh-sh!' said the native doctor, nodding towards the front gate. 'There he comes.'

Coming through the door was a small boy of fourteen, slim, black and shiny as a young eel. His resemblance to his father was striking. He had a sweet small face that made you think what a beautiful little boy his father must have been, too, at fourteen. His lips were slightly parted and his teeth glittered between them like lightning between dark clouds. Apart from a pair of ragged pants, he was naked and barefooted. On his head was a clay pot, full of water, and supporting this was a semi-dry banana leaf wound into a soft wheel to constitute a head-protecting pad. He had such captivating features that we couldn't help smiling as he approached.

'Well, whaddya know!' exclaimed Dicky in his friendliest voice. 'So this is the young friend I've been waiting for!'

The boy eyed his father shyly.

'We've got visitors, son,' the native doctor said. 'Go and put your pot down. At the usual place in the back-yard. Then you can come back here and hear what our white friend has to say.'

Silent as ever, the boy obeyed and took his pot behind the house.

'You've got quite a boy there,' said Dicky when the boy was gone. 'Sharp brilliant eyes and athletic possibilities. All he needs is opportunity. If only you'll let me handle him.'

'You'll have all the opportunity you need, presently,' replied Okwologu and suddenly: 'Ah – there he comes. Come over here, son.' The boy had returned, no longer carrying the pot. His hair was short and curly and stood like beads about his ears.

Here and there, his body had patches of wetness which indicated he had been having a swim. He stood by his father's side, leaning against his shoulder.

'Hello, young man,' Dicky began confidently, 'I've come to see you. I'm your friend.' The boy smiled shyly. 'I've come from America and I've brought you some aeroplanes to play with.' Dicky produced two toys. 'There, what d'you say?'

'You know he can't talk,' said the boy's father. 'His tongue is sore and swollen.'

'Of course, of course,' replied Dicky, still addressing the boy. 'I hear you're not well, so I've brought you a white girl-friend to look after you. Here she is.' Dicky produced a doll from his pocket. 'You can see she's smiling at you. She loves you and wants to take care of you. And, believe it or not, there's plenty more where she came from. At my hospital. They're all waiting to welcome you there. So you see, you're quite a popular young man. In my hospital, you could have as many women like this one as you like, so beautiful that the village chief and all his wives will be jealous of you. What d'you say, boy? Oh – I remember, you can't talk. How about coming to an agreement? Because your tongue hurts you, we don't want to make it worse, do we? So, we must find another means of making ourselves understood, mustn't we? Yes, I know! When I ask you a question, nod your head for "Yes" and shake it for "No". Right?'

'Yes, he can do that,' replied the boy's father.

'Excellent,' said Dicky, smiling. 'Now, would you like to come over here and take your aeroplanes?'

The boy shook his head. For a moment, Dicky forgot to smile but remembered soon enough for his next question.

'How about this lovely white girl-friend?'

The boy indicated 'No'.

Dicky looked at me helplessly, I shrugged my shoulders, indicating that I did not want to become involved in this.

'Well,' Dicky went on, smiling at the boy once more. 'Perhaps you're right. Maybe toys and dolls are a little childish for

78

you. But don't despair. I've brought you something else. Candies. Do you know what they are? Delicious to eat.' He ate one himself.

'Don't worry,' said the boy's father. 'My son knows what your candies are. Especially to the teeth.'

Dicky ignored the remark.

'Well, my friend?' he continued. 'Would you like some candies?'

The boy shook his head.

'Listen to me, boy. If you come to the hospital with me, I'll send you to school, to the university, to England and America, to the land of great learning. And when you come back here, you'll have lots of money and big American cars. Instead of living in this old tin house, you'll have mansions. One for your father, one for yourself, one for your wife and kids. Then everyone will say: this is the sensible boy who's made his family name far greater than even his father dreamed he would. I promise you that —'

Okwologu interrupted: 'I thought it was your Church that said: Man does not live by bread alone. You're just tempting my boy like the devil tempted the son of your God.'

Dicky ignored the interruption as before. He went on: 'You'll then be a doctor who can read and write. Yes, you can write books then if you like. Like my friend, Obi.' Dicky slapped me affectionately on the back. 'He was an ignorant little African boy before. Just like you. But he's been to England to study and returned. Now he writes books and travels in aeroplanes. Real ones.' Needless to add, another guttural noise escaped me. But Dicky went on unaffected. 'You can even become a prime minister. Just think of it! A prime minister. Now, will you come?'

The boy, still expressionless, shook his head as before.

'Look here, you little brat.' Dicky had lost his temper. 'If you refuse to come with me to the hospital, you'll die. Do you know that?'

The boy raised his eyebrows as if to say: 'Really! How nice!'

'If you don't come,' Dicky was furious, 'I'll report you and your father to the police. You'll be arrested, tried by the big judge, not the chief, but the big judge with long grey hair, and then you'll be sent to prison. If that happens, you can't be a witch doctor any more.'

'How like the white man!' countered the native doctor. 'You're all the same. First you befriend. Then you advise. Then you suggest. Then you bribe. Then you insist. Then you threaten. Then you force. Then you arrest. Then you imprison. Then you destroy.'

'Oh, hell!'

'Please don't use bad language before my son. I don't want him to grow up like you — if you're really grown up — arrogant white man who knows nothing about life except that he belongs to a superior stock. You speak about big jobs, big cars, big houses. In this part of the world, such things don't count. Do you know why? Because we believe in peace and happiness. Happiness doesn't mean power of property. It's a state of a good man's mind. So, to be happy, you must first of all be good. And to feel good, you don't extort to amass wealth, you give to the have-nots. The happiest moments of my life have been spent in isolation, in faraway hills and valleys of green grass. I just sit there quietly and watch the trees grow new bark and the grass grow greener with the caress of sunshine. Do you understand that? Of course you don't understand. I don't expect you to understand. You're young, you're arrogant, you're white. How can you understand? You've been in a hurry all your life; like a man pursued by an evil spirit. Maybe that's what it is. You are perpetually chased by evil spirits. They only torture those who torture their fellow human beings. Please leave my son alone. He believes in the power of the spirits. They love him. They teach him. They give him the secret of love and happiness. That's why he's not in a hurry and at war with life like you. Please don't make a soldier out of my son. He has no enemies to fight, life least of all.'

After the doctor's tirade, Dicky made one last effort to win over the boy.

'Look here, my little friend,' he said, 'I want you to come

with me because it's good for you. The big white doctor wants
you to come. Dr Williams. You know Dr Williams, don't you?'

The boy nodded his head and smiled. This encouraged
Dicky.

'Then will you come?'

The boy frowned once more and shook his head.

'Oh, what's the use!'

'Well,' Okwologu said, 'if you've finished with my son, he has
to rest now. Don't forget he's not well.' And, patting the boy on
the head, he said, 'You can go now, son. Go and have a lie down.'

The boy nodded, smiled shyly once more, and went into the
house. This was a signal for the two men to renew their argument.

'You leave us no choice but to take the boy by force,'
Dicky warned the native doctor.

'I cannot read and write,' replied Okwologu, 'but I do know
my rights, you know. I'm his father. You cannot take him from
here without my consent.'

'You're very wrong there, old man. In the case of mad
parents — and any doctor who does not certify you as one must
be mad himself — in an extreme case like this one, the authorities
concerned can disregard parental objection. What the hell's
amusing you now?'

Okwologu shook his head slowly, his mysterious roguish
smile shining through his beard.

'You're a big baby, aren't you, son?'

'You may laugh now,' said Dicky angrily. 'You won't find it
so funny when the Police Inspector gets here, I promise you that.'

Okwologu burst into a hearty laughter. It was like looking
into the mouth of a roaring lion. A chill went through me and, if
Dicky's expression was a good guide, through him too. There was
something terribly mysterious about this man, Okwologu. Perhaps,
as Dicky suggested, he was going mad. So I thought, but dared say
nothing. From the way he was looking at us with his red eyes
burning, it was plain he had lost whatever little respect he had for
us when we first entered his premises. I was beginning to feel

81

restive when, to my great relief, someone knocked at the front gate. As we turned, a short fat old man walked into the yard. White but badly sunburnt, he was wearing an old tropical suit and a Churchillian white hat.

'Dr Williams!' Dicky exclaimed in surprise.

Okwologu, smiling broadly, rose from his stool and stepped forward to meet the new visitor. They shook hands vigorously.

'And how's my old friend today?' said Dr Williams.

'It's nice to see you, Dr Williams,' Okwologu replied. 'Welcome to my house.'

'I've brought you a present, friend.'

'Yes? Let me guess. Whisky?'

'Cunning fox!' Dr Williams laughed.

'And I've got no palm-wine for you in the house. You didn't tell me you were coming today.'

'Never mind. Some other time.'

'And where's the whisky? Don't tell me. Let me guess. You've forgotten to take it out of the car as usual? And the car's parked just outside?'

'As a matter of fact, yes,' said Dr Williams, laughing again, 'I must really do something about my memory one of these days.'

'Never mind, Dr Williams. I'll go and take it from the car.'

'Will you? Good. The car's under the oil-bean tree. The tall one. Not the short one today. I came from the other direction.'

'I see. I won't be long.'

Okwologu left us and went to collect his drink. Dr Williams sat down and stretched his legs.

'Well, Dicky,' he said, 'what are you doing here? Or are you a friend of my native doctor friend too?'

'What kind of question is that?' asked Dicky. 'You know what I'm doing here, Dr Williams.'

'I haven't the faintest idea, young man. In fact I was surprised to see your car parked outside.'

'Didn't you come here to look for me then?'

'No, I merely dropped in to say hello to my old friend. How

82

should I know you were here?'

'But you sent me here, Dr Williams.'

'Did I? I can't remember asking you to do that. Why should I send you when I was planning to pay him a visit myself today anyway?'

'But you did, Dr Williams. Don't you remember?'

'Remember what, Dicky?'

'That you asked me to come and persuade him about his son.'

'Which son?'

'The one with the tongue infection. So, I asked my way here.'

Dr Williams burst out laughing.

'So that was what happened,' he said. 'I'm sorry, Dicky, it's all a mistake. My fault, really.'

'What's your fault, Dr Williams?'

'I ought to have told you that there are two men who go by the name of Okwologu in this village. There is Okwologu, the carpenter who lives further down the tarred road, and there is my friend, Okwologu the native doctor. I sent you to the other fellow, Okwologu the carpenter, not Okwologu the native doctor. Your guides must have misled you because the native doctor is the better known.'

'Then I'm mighty glad I was misled,' said Dicky. 'Because I came to the right place after all.'

'I'm sorry,' said Dr Williams, 'I'm not with you. What d'you mean you've come to the right place after all?'

'Whoever gave the information must have confused the two chaps too. You ought to have sent me here, to this Okwologu in actual fact, not to the other bloke.'

'How can it be when the carpenter's son was admitted to the hospital a few minutes ago?'

'No, it is the native doctor's son who has the tongue infection. You've admitted the wrong boy.'

Dr Williams frowned.

'Did you say the native doctor's son?' he asked.

83

'Yes.'

'You must be joking, young man.'

'But I'm not, Dr Williams.'

'Dicky! Okwologu, the native doctor, has no son. He hasn't even got a wife.'

'Dr Williams, it's you who's joking. The man has a son.'

'Listen to me, young man. Okwologu has been my close friend for over twenty years. I can bet you anything he hasn't got a child, male or female, he's not even married.'

'But he must have a son,' said Dicky, looking at me to prove he had a witness. 'We saw the boy, didn't we, Obi?'

I nodded.

'We were right here when the boy came back from the stream. He came right through that door, didn't he?'

I nodded.

'He went behind the house, put down his tin of water, and came out here, right again, Obi?'

I shook my head.

'What do you mean: no?' Dicky hollered at me.

'He wasn't carrying a tin,' I said quietly, 'he was carrying a pot, a small brown clay pot, similar to the one I used to have when I was his age.'

'It's not true,' Dicky retorted vehemently. 'It was a tin, a disused old kerosene tin, like the cook's little boy at the hospital used to carry up and down to the stream. That's what made me take special note of it.'

'I still think it was a clay pot,' I said.

'And I say it was a tin. You wanna bet?' Dicky plunged his hand into his pocket, rattling the coins in it.

'Come on, boys,' said Dr Williams, 'behave yourselves. Don't make an issue out of what the boy was carrying. The important question is whether or not Okwologu has a son.'

'Of course he has a son,' Dicky said heatedly. 'We both saw him, didn't we? Okay, we disagree about what he was carrying but, like you said yourself, Dr Williams, the important thing is whether the boy was here or not. And we tell you he was. See,' nd he kicked the toys with his boot, 'I've been offering him dolls nd candies to make him follow me to the hospital, but it didn't work. Not long before you arrived, Doctor.'

'Incredible!' exclaimed Dr Williams. 'Where's the boy now?'

'He went into the house, didn't he, Obi?'

I nodded.

'He's in that room over there. Why don't you see for ourself, doctor?'

'I will.' The round figure of Dr Williams rolled into the ouse and after a long search re-emerged again.

'Well?' said the American.

'Dicky,' Dr Williams said indignantly, 'is this some kind of April fool or what? This is February, young man, in case you've orgotten.'

'What is all that about?' Dicky asked.

'There's not a soul in that house,' exploded Dr Williams. 'Not even a bloody fly.'

'Come, come, now, Dr Williams. I know you've a touch of stigmatism, but this is stark ridiculous. If you can't see a boy hat size, then you really ought to see a doctor.'

'I take it that you're implying you can find the boy yourself?'

'Certainly. I'll fetch the stubborn rascal out for you. Excuse ne.'

Dicky went into the house and, after another intense ummaging, came out, looking bewildered.

'Well?' It was Dr Williams's turn to ask.

'He's not there,' Dicky replied. 'Nowhere in the house.'

To satisfy my curiosity, I went into the house also, looked verywhere, and met with no better success.

'Are you serious about seeing the boy?' Dr Williams asked.

'Of course I am,' Dicky replied.

'And Okwologu, did he see him too?'

'Yes, he did. He spoke to him all the time, calling him "Son."'

'You said the boy came back from the stream, carrying, er —

85

a water container?'

'Yes.'

'Where did he put this water container?'

'Yes,' exclaimed Dicky exultantly, 'that will prove me right. He put the tin behind the house, in the back-yard.'

'Shall we go and see for ourselves then?' said Dr Williams.

But the only things we found behind the house were two empty giant-sized black clay pots, so thick and heavy that no small boy could have lifted them from the ground. It would take a man of Okwologu's physique and energy to carry them on his head when they were full of water.

'Well, Dicky,' said Dr Williams, 'where's the tin of water you were telling me about?' and turning to me, 'Or did you say it was a little brown clay pot?'

We were still arguing about it when Okwologu himself arrived, carrying a bottle of whisky under his arm.

'Ah — you're here, Okwologu,' said Dr Williams. 'What's all this I hear about your having a son?'

'Yes,' rejoined Dicky, 'tell Dr Williams about your son. He won't believe me. And we can't find the boy anywhere. Tell the doctor the boy's here. He's got to be. We saw him. We spoke to him. Ask him to come.'

But the native doctor only grinned at Dr Williams, a glint of mischief in his eyes.'

'Your friend's a big baby, Dr Williams,' he said casually. 'He's quite a lot to learn about Africa.' And clamping the neck of the bottle between his teeth, he crushed it with one bite, spitting out the pieces of broken glass on the ground. Then he began to pour the content of the bottle into his gullet.

Dr Williams nodded his head understandingly, a faint smile creeping over his face.

'I understand, my friend,' he said to the native doctor, 'I do understand indeed. Have a good drink.'

'What was all that about?' Dicky asked.

'I think I know what happened,' answered Dr Williams,

miling broadly.

'What happened?' Dicky's face was all impatience.

'Did you have an argument with Okwologu? Particularly with egard to his mystic powers?'

'Yes, I did give him a few home truths about his witch-loctoring buffoonery. He can't even explain the behaviour of his own medicine, if you can call this concoction medicine, in lementary technical language. And I told him so.'

'From now onwards you'll know better, of course?'

'Meaning what, Dr Williams?'

'Just this, Dicky. That you'll respect genius wherever you ind it, even in an African witch doctor.'

'Respect a witch doctor as a genius?' Dicky was highly mused. 'Really? And why, may I ask?'

'You just told me you saw a little boy?'

'Because I most certainly did, Dr Williams.'

'Did this boy speak?'

'No.'

'Did you touch him?'

'No.'

'Did he touch you?'

'No.'

'There's your answer, Dicky.'

'Meaning precisely what, Dr Williams?'

'Meaning that this witch doctor, as you persist in calling im, has just done what all the eminent medical scientists of the 'est put together cannot explain. And probably never will.'

'And what has he done?'

'In elementary technical language, Dicky, this man has just reated imagination.'

DAUGHTERS OF THE SUN

The old woman glared at the setting sun. It did not hurt her eyes; for those watering eyeballs had long been shaded by age. She was not leaning on purpose either; she was standing as erect as the weight of years would let her. Her body was wrinkled, her hair long and scraggy, but clean. The river rolled like an angry cloud past her feet, thrashing the opposite shores and, where it descended a precipice further down the course, roaring a war song as if in mockery of her helplessness.

'*Nono,*' meaning 'Great Lady', 'are you all right?'

The old lady turned. A man was standing in the middle of the bridge. This consisted of long bamboo stems tied end to end with tough strings made from palm fibre. On either side of the bridge, long wooden poles were stuck into the river-bed at regular intervals as support for those who had not mastered the art of crossing a bamboo bridge. During the rainy season, almost everybody needed this support, for the river overflowed the bridge and travellers had to clutch the poles with both hands while their feet traced the bridge line like a blind man's stick through the muddy and angry waves. Tonight, however, it was different. The water level was far beneath the crossing, and the sturdy legs of the tall stranger were in no danger of getting wet. The sky was cloudless and the breeze wafted the scent of water lilies through lacy openings in the forest.

'Did you talk to me, young man?' asked the old lady, her voice strong and twenty years younger than the body that gave it source. 'Speak up. I'm half deaf.'

The 'young man' was well over forty, towering in height but slightly hunched. From the Ichi engravings on his face, you could see that he had already secured his Ozo title which, considering his age, spoke well for his tenacity of purpose and industry. If he

89

kept on at such a pace, he might even make the Eze-Udu rank in about five years. It was difficult, though, to imagine this man's ankle wearing the great Udu chaplets at the tender age of fifty. His wrapper was new, his jumpa just as new, and the Obejili knife in his hand heavy and sharp. His face broke into a smile.

'I said, Great Lady,' he repeated loudly, 'are you all right? Can I help you in any way?'

'Ekene,' muttered the old lady, meaning 'Heaven be blest', 'the gods have sent me someone at last.'

'Do you want something done, Great Lady?'

'Yes, son. Could you help me lift this pot to my head?' The man saw a dotted clay pot standing on the water weeds; it had been filled with water from the spring. 'I came down to the stream when the sun was still high in the sky, level with the top of that tree over there. Now it's almost swallowed up by the heavenly ocean.'

'And you've waited that long?'

'Yes. No one has passed this way since. It must be the farming season. Everyone's on the farm. If I had known the river would be deserted, I would have brought a smaller pitcher to fetch the water, a calabash maybe, so that I wouldn't have to stand here and wait for someone to help me.'

'Don't worry, Great Lady. You won't wait any longer. I am here.'

The man came down the bridge, rolled the lower end of his wrapper, and waded into the water. But when he jolted the pot, he let out an exclamation.

'Ekh! Were you going to carry this on your head, Great Lady?'

'Yes. Why not?'

'It's like lifting the earth itself! Far too heavy for a frail lady like you.'

'But what else can I do?'

'How far do you live from here?'

'Just up the hill, between Ezanyidogo and Ez'anekwu.'

'Well, in that case,' said the man smiling, even though neither

90

name meant anything to him, 'perhaps you'll do me the great
honour of letting me take the water home for you before I
continue with my journey?'

'Thank you, young man. I knew you were a true African
the moment I set eyes on you. Strong as a lion, black as a god,
kind as a grandmother.'

'Shall we start, Lady?'

'Why not, son? Why not?'

The old lady picked her walking stick off the grass,
tightened her wrapper over her breasts, and hobbled forward. The
man, carrying the pot on his head, led the way. The river growled
behind them as if grudging their departure. About once a month,
the women of the village, summoned by a gong, came down
here together to give the river a thorough cleaning, weeding the
banks, clearing the river-beds of rubbish, especially the broken
pots and bottles which endangered swimmers. The women gossiped,
chanted, and played as they worked. In a way, it was a sort of
merry-making for them and what you might call an unofficial
house of parliament where housewives enacted new bills affecting
domestic life and made sure that these applied in every home.
They called this regular stream-cleaning *Igwo Mmili*. The erection
of new bridges at yearly intervals and the construction of the
main road leading to the river were the men's responsibility. But
the present condition of the river did not show much evidence of
this kind of treatment. From the heaps of bitter leaf stalks left
here and there, the slime and grime of bread-fruits, and the stench
of rotting cassava left-overs, it was evident that the sowing season
had kept everybody in the farm, away from *Igwo Mmili* chores
and pleasures. The wind blew from behind, sweeping through the
bushes and filling the man's nostrils with moist air. He sneezed
and turned round to see how the old lady was progressing. But
she was not coming behind him as he had thought. She had
stopped further down the road and was standing on an old tree
stump, gazing at the setting sun as before.

'What's the matter, Great Lady?' the man asked. 'Why

aren't you coming?'

'It's sad, really,' she replied, shaking her head.

'What's sad?'

'Not being able to see them tonight. They must have gone over the other side of the sun.'

'Of whom do you speak, Great Lady?'

'You ask questions like a child. I speak of the daughters of the sun, of course.'

'All strangers ask questions like a child, madam. Forgive me, but I've never heard of the daughters of the sun.'

'Never?' The old lady was so shocked by this admission that she rolled her eyes till they nearly fell from their sockets. 'You must come from a far-away land indeed.'

'I do, Great Lady. I'm a traveller by profession, a collector of legends. All I know about this town is that your god is Ogwugwu and that Nwachukwu, the great artist, lived here. And I must not forget Ezeoku, the mighty warrior.'

'How little you know about us, good stranger!' the old lady said with a little laugh.

'Would you tell me about the daughters of the sun?'

'If you collect legends, my dear man, that story is not your kind of wine. It's a true story if ever there was one.'

'Then I am all the more intrigued. I pay well, you know.'

'I'd rather drop into a well than take a cowrie from you. You paid for my story when you offered to carry that pot home for me. You're a good man. Never take money from a good man, my mother used to say; it pays better to share their goodness with them instead. I will tell you a story that will make your ears smart. But first we must be on our way; for the sun's half asleep and soon it will be darker than dark.'

'I'm listening, Great Lady,' he said, leading the way once more. 'So make my ears smart with your strange tale.'

The sky above him was like blue silk, in which the stars were already making an appearance. And the old lady began her narrative, thumping the hard soil with her stick in time with the rise and fall

92

of her voice:

'Many many years ago, when men were men and woman were
women, when maids had breasts and stayed as pretty as nature made
them, when men, like giants, were so wrapped in muscles and so
proud of this that they dared not hide their thighs in cotton as they
do today, it was then, my dear stranger, that such things as I am about
to tell you could happen. Far, far away from here, beyond the
white hills of Okija, there was a little quiet village. It had only one
inhabitant. He was a hunter. No one knew his name, who he was, why
he lived there, or even where he came from. It was impossible to tell
because he was uncommunicative. People from neighbouring villages
saw him only when he came to sell elephant tusks and leopard skins.
He was big and ugly and had more scars on his body than he had hairs.

'Brave Hunter, Brave Hunter,' people would call, 'why do
you live alone, Brave Hunter?' In reply he would only shrug his
shoulders. Then they would offer him some drink, knowing full
well he would never touch it.

'If you insult me once more with your palm-wine, I will
swallow the insult,' the hunter would threaten amidst a roar of
laughter. This was the only joke he knew and the single proof
that he was not dumb. In those days, bravery was like bride-price.
Young women flung themselves at him and fathers would bring
their most beautiful daughters to introduce to him. But the
hunter showed no interest at all. With a shrug of his shoulders, he
soon indicated that the interview was over, neither women nor
wine interested him.

'Brave Hunter, Brave Hunter,' a father would plead, 'why
won't you get married, Brave Hunter?' To this the hunter's answer
was another shrug of the shoulders and home he would go to his
village in the hills.

The roof of the house where he lived was made from the
skins of various animals, the walls of elephant tusks and,
surrounding the house itself, was a fence of lion teeth. So many
animals had he killed! Even the cup he drank from was the skull

93

of a monkey. Oh, he was such a great man! A real giant among men!

However, the hunter had one formidable enemy: boredom. Since he hated wine, women, and dancing, the only thing that gave him pleasure in life was hunting. But now, even that bored him. He had killed every kind of animal that there was to be killed, and himself had nothing left to live for. He became very sad and would grind his teeth from cockcrow to nightfall.

One day, an idea struck him. Why not go in search of some kind of animal he had never killed before? There must be one somewhere, and even if there wasn't, the mere search for it would cure his boredom. Surely, he reflected, there *must* be an animal that man had never heard of. This idea excited the hunter greatly. He remembered tales about the Forest of Reincarnation. The very thought of this place made him shiver like a child in a cold wind. Legend had it that the forest was the land of the dead and that no human being had ever penetrated it. Those who had attempted to do so had never emerged alive. Tales about this notorious forest were brought by travellers from distant lands. Why not make history, he thought, by going there to hunt? Yes! Why hadn't he thought of it before?

A few days later, the brave hunter set out with his gun and equipment. He crossed seven lands and seven seas before he reached his destination, a forest as forbidding as the travellers had said. From a distance, it looked smoky and unearthly and, as you came nearer to it, you had a strange feeling that a one-eyed man was staring at you fixedly and that the entire forest constituted this eye, the rest of the face being invisible. Stepping into the forest was like passing through the magic curtain of Umualiisi. The hunter's heart was filled with premonition. All at once he saw a thick cloud cross the sky, covering the forest, and, for a time, he thought he heard bells ringing. But all soon became calm and quiet once more. Not that these portents mattered in the least, for danger was an irresistible attraction to this man.

He walked on and on, turning neither right nor left, as if a force was pulling him forward. The strangest thing of all was that there were no animals in the forest, not even a worm in the soil. Here and there were the bones and feathers of birds that had lost their way and made the mistake of trying to fly over the Forest of Reincarnation. The hunter continued walking until he came to the other edge of the forest, which, to his amazement, concealed a large expanse of water, a sea so vast and green that he nearly fell into it with dizziness. He was about to turn away when he saw something approaching in the distance. It rolled on the surface of the water like a ball of fire and was coming directly towards him. Filled with panic, the hunter ran to the nearest tree and, climbing to the top, hid himself among the leaves. From here, he watched and waited to see what would happen next.

The rolling flame came nearer the edge of the forest and stopped. It split in two with a loud noise, revealing at its centre a boat carrying two girls. The hunter nearly fell from his tree at the sight of such beauty. The boat was made of gold and the maids inside it were as brown as honey. They looked exactly alike, so beautiful and dusky that they dimmed the stars above with their sombre glow. Their hair circled like fresh raffia and breasts stood out on their chests like the tower bells of Arabbi. They looked around carefully to make certain that there was nobody there. The hunter held his breath. Convinced that they were alone, one of the girls said to the other:

'Now, sister, you first.'

The other one stood up and began her strange declaration.

'I, one of the twin daughters of the sun, hereby declare that I am going to the world of men on a fifteen-year holiday. In exactly nine months from now, I will be born in the town of Awkuzu to a woman called Oyemma. My parents are very rich and have already three male children. I will be their fourth and last child, and the only daughter of the family. My parents will spoil me and I will grow up a beautiful naughty girl and the envy of the town. But on my fourteenth birthday, there will be a storm and a branch will fall off the tree in our front yard. It will strike me down instantly and kill me on the spot. I will shed my mortal flesh as soon as I am buried and come straight back here to the boat to wait for my sister. All this I swear in the name of our father, the grand sun.'

As she finished, she nodded at her sister and sat down. The other stood up and spoke:

'I, one of the twin daughters of the sun, hereby declare that I am going to the world of men on a seventeen-year holiday. In exactly nine months from today I will be born as a baby girl at a village called Okija. My father is an old farmer called Obidile and my mother's name is Akuedu. They are both seventy and they have no children. My hope is to keep them company for sixteen years and make them as happy as they have a right to be. On my sixteenth birthday, I will ask my father to buy me an ox for a present. Three days later it will trample me to death. I will shed my mortal flesh as soon as I am buried and come back here at sunrise to rejoin my dear sister for our return journey to our planet of origin, the sun. All this I swear in the name of our father, the grand sun.'

When she had finished, both sisters got off the boat and walked into the forest silently. They took about twelve paces and stopped.

'Promise you will be here, sister,' said one to the other.

'I promise.'

'And that nothing will keep you.'

'I promise. And you too.'

'I promise, sister, I promise.'

Then they walked into a clearing and disappeared.

The hunter came down from the tree and ran all the way home. The village of Okija in which the second of the twin sisters said she would be reincarnated was only a mile from his home. So he set out for Okija with a large pot of palm wine. When he got there, he asked for an old couple called Obidile and Akuedu.

'Brave Hunter, Brave Hunter,' the villagers called, 'what do you want with a dying old husband and wife? We thought you didn't drink but now you're carrying a pot. They're sterile and have no daughter for you to marry. Why bother with them, Brave Hunter?'

To this, as usual, he shrugged his shoulders, and the villagers, burning with jealousy and curiosity, led him to the old couple. The hunter, a man of few words even at a time like this, said what he wanted briefly:

'I have come to ask the hand of your daughter in marriage.'

'Brave Hunter, Brave Hunter,' said the old couple, 'we have been married for fifty years but no child has come our way.'

'I know you have no child,' said the hunter. 'I also know you are going to have a baby girl in nine months' time. She will be as beautiful as sunset and no one is going to marry her but me.'

'Brave Hunter, Brave Hunter, you do the strangest of things, but what you say now is even stranger than your deeds,' the old man replied. 'We're too old to have a child. We couldn't succeed when we were young and full of seeds. How can we now?'

'Leave that to destiny, my friends. Take my word for its usual worth. Have I not killed elephants when I said I would, and shot lions stronger than strong? Why doubt me now?'

'Brave Hunter, Brave Hunter, what you are predicting is a miracle, not an act of bravery. You may be brave, but you are not a god. How do you come by such information?'

The hunter merely shrugged his shoulders and smiled. He was misunderstood by his hosts.

'He's laughing at us,' the couple said. 'Are you not ashamed of yourself? Do you not get enough amusement from jesting monkeys and chimps that you should go about laughing at childless old people in their homes? Have you no respect for age and misfortune?'

They took broomsticks and chased the hunter out of their home. He could have knocked them both down with a wave of his hand but he restrained himself. Disappointed but not dismayed, he returned to his house and waited patiently.

Five months later, he had a visit from Obidile, the old man.

'Brave Hunter, Brave Hunter,' the old man shouted from the

97

door, 'your prophecy has come true. My wife's going to have a baby. Not long now! She's five months pregnant already.'

'Five months!' said the hunter. 'Why didn't you come to tell me earlier?'

'Because we didn't know what it was at first. When her womb began to bulge, we thought it was food poisoning of some sort and hoped she would get over it. But it got worse and bigger and we had to go to Okwologu, the native doctor. He found it difficult to believe it possible in a woman of seventy but, there you are, he confirmed this morning that Akuedu, my wife, is in fact pregnant. You're a man of vision indeed, Brave Hunter. How come the gods have endowed you with bravery and vision when most men are denied both?'

The hunter shrugged his shoulders.

Four months later, the baby was born.

'Brave Hunter, Brave Hunter,' the messenger from Okija called, 'I've come from Obidile, the old farmer. He says to tell you his wife has just given birth to your wife. And will you come with me at once.'

The hunter took the pot of palm-wine which he had already secured for the occasion and hastened to Okija. There was great rejoicing when he got there. He at once recognized the baby's face as a smaller version of the one he had seen in the Forest of Reincarnation. Everybody commented on how beautiful the baby was as the hunter lifted her up.

'Yes, very beautiful, I agree,' said the hunter. 'A true daughter of the sun indeed.'

At this the baby burst out crying, kicking her little hands and feet into the air.

'What have you done to her, Brave Hunter?' someone asked. 'She cries as if she'd been stung by a scorpion.'

'I could have sworn I saw her open her eyes then,' said another, 'and swoon at you before she began to cry. What have you done to her?'

'Don't let our gestures distress you, my friends,' said the

hunter. 'Just an ordinary husband and wife quarrel.' This evoked peals of laughter from everyone standing round.

'Brave Hunter, Brave Hunter,' the old farmer called, 'because of what you've done for us and the baby, we've decided to call her *Dintajaanu,* which means: Betrothed to the Brave Hunter.'

The hunter shook his head.

'No, my dear father-in-law,' he said. 'A name like that is apt to embarrass us in years to come when I am too old to hunt and too frail to be called brave.'

'What name do you suggest instead?'

The hunter thought for a while and said:

'Why don't we just call her Ejima?'

'Ejima!' exclaimed the bewildered old man. 'But Ejima means Twins. Why give her a name like that when she's single? And see, the baby is crying loudly again as if even she disapproves of the name.'

'You know better than to argue with me, don't you?' said the hunter, ignoring the baby's wailing.

'Anything you say, Brave Hunter, anything you say. We'll call her Ejima.'

'And talking of arguing, I want to make one stipulation here and now concerning this child.'

'What's that?' asked the old couple.

'That under no circumstances — and I repeat under no circumstances — must an ox be brought into this compound, either for sale or as a present.'

'An ox!' exclaimed the old man, chuckling. 'What a strange request to make!'

'I'm not laughing, old man. And I don't care what kind of request it is, but I want it carried out implicitly. No ox, do you hear me?'

'All right, Brave Hunter,' said the old man. 'No ox in my house. I promise you that.'

From that day onwards, the baby cried every time the hunter paid a visit.

99

'Brave Hunter, Brave Hunter,' people often said, 'why is it this child dislikes you so much?' to which the hunter invariably gave the same response, a shrug of the shoulders.

The years rolled by. Ejima grew into a lovely young woman. Her beauty was the talk of the town, people came from far and near just to set eyes on her, and not one regretted the journey. On the contrary, they all marvelled at what they saw and swore to come back some day. Her parents loved her more than anything in the world. The parental affection which had been lying dormant in them for forty years was expended on her. They gave her everything she wanted and wished she would ask for more. But Ejima had everything a girl could ask for and was well pleased with life. She grew tall beyond her years, robust in the right places, generous with her smiles to everyone but the hunter. She did not grow out of her hatred for him. Indeed, it increased until it became a paralysing phobia. She avoided his eyes like lightning and would never mention his name. Whenever he called at the house, she would either pick up the pot and run down to the stream or take the rope and go to fetch firewood. She would not come back for hours on end and, when she did at last, would stop outside the door and listen for a while to make sure the hunter was gone before she ventured into the yard. These rebuffs did not worry him unduly. He waited patiently, biding his time. The only thing he did was to remind her parents from time to time about not allowing any ox into the compound. The old couple maintained that this was an easy promise to keep, asking proudly: Hadn't they kept it all these years?

However, Ejima's sixteenth birthday came at last. She got up very early in the morning and went to her parents.

'What do you want, Ejima?' they asked. 'You've got that sad look on your face.'

'Father and mother,' she said, 'you know that I've never really begged you for anything.'

'We know that, child. Why do you ask?'

'Because, for the first time in my life, I want something

100

badly.'

'Of course, child,' they said, stroking her hands fondly. 'Ask anything you want. Isn't today your birthday? We'll give you anything you name. Now, tell us what it is you want.'

'An ox,' replied Ejima curtly.

Her parents jumped out of bed.

'What did you say?' asked the old man.

'I said I want an ox, father.'

'Well now, child, er, look, don't you think that an ox is an odd present for a girl?'

'Not if the girl wants it as much as I do. And is fortunate enough to have very loving parents as I do.'

'Yes, you know we love you, child. But you've asked for the one present you can't have.'

'Why can't I have it, father?'

But the old couple had promised the hunter to keep their mouths shut. Even if they hadn't, they still wouldn't know what to say, for the hunter had kept the real secret to himself. Ejima cried all day and all night. She knew how soft-hearted her parents were and that every drop of her tears was like a spear thrust through their hearts. She had also refused to eat, not even a tiny cube of Mbili, a special delicacy which her parents always prepared for her on grand occasions.

Early the next day, the old man went to see the hunter and told him what was going on.

'Brave Hunter, Brave Hunter,' he cried in conclusion, 'the poor girl is going to starve herself to death. Surely you don't want to be married to a corpse. What are we going to do, Brave Hunter?'

'Let her starve,' was all the answer he got. The hunter was as immovable as a rock.

'I've heard rumours that your mother mated with a lion when you were conceived. When you talk like this, I wonder whether it wasn't a scorpion. You're all sting and no heart. What do you gain by refusing your own fiancée a present of her choice? Sometimes I wonder if you love her at all. You've not even given

101

her any present this birthday.'

'The greatest present anyone can ever give your daughter is that refusal. And as her fiancé, I claim the sole privilege and the responsibility of making it.'

More confused than ever, the old man took the bad news home to his wife. They waited another day and another night, but no change came. Ejima still locked herself up in her room, crying and starving. This was too much for them, their one and only daughter crying her heart out like that! They talked about it all night and began to question the good will of the hunter, this man who was so devoid of human love that he had to build himself an isolated village to become a recluse, a man so used to killing that he had even killed the instinct of loving in himself. Who was he, anyway? Just a man with a gun! No one knew who he really was, what he was, or where he came from. Confronted with a choice between him and their loving daughter, why choose the stranger? This was equivalent to betrayal! Whoever heard of parents betraying their own daughter to appease an eccentric stranger? Yes, the hunter was an evil man! Why did they bother to listen to him in the first place? He was dictatorial, conceited, and wicked. He was a monster! Thanks to the gods that this incident had happened just in time to let them realize to what a beast they nearly married their one and only daughter! What was so unique about this hunter detecting the pregnancy before them? He was young, his sight was sound, he might even have had some experience in his past about these things, perhaps he was a widower. If they had been as young and experienced as he was, they might just as easily have detected that Akuedu was pregnant early enough, even before the hunter had done so. Predicting pregnancy indeed! What a flimsy excuse on which to base a marriage! No, their daughter was not going to marry the hunter. How heartless of them, they said, even to contemplate it. She would have the ox she asked for and the hunter could jump into the nearest ocean and play with the sharks! But the old couple only said these things because they wanted an excuse for their

102

weakness. In their hearts, they knew they still loved and reverenced
the hunter and in fact admired his determination.

At the first cockcrow the next dawn, the old man hurried to
a place in the neighbourhood where a few Hausa nomads were
spending the night with their flock. Unable to wait in case he
changed his mind again, he got the nomads out of their tents and
made his purchase. Taking the ox home, he called out to Ejima
that her present had arrived and that she should come and look.
Ejima and her mother ran out of the house, screaming with joy.
Ejima was so excited that she slapped the ox on the eye. The
animal panicked, rushed forward, and trampled her underfoot.
She died before her parents could lift her up.

'Brave Hunter, Brave Hunter,' the old man cried, kneeling
down in shame, 'I have brought you bad tidings. Ejima, our
lovely daughter, your beloved wife-to-be, is, is dead.'

'Did you disobey my orders?' shouted the hunter, wearing
a killer's frown. 'Did you buy her that ox?'

'I'm afraid so, Brave Hunter. She was only playing with the
ox when she —'

'Don't tell me how she died. I know. Get back home and
stay there till I return.'

'Where are you going, Brave Hunter?'

The hunter shrugged his shoulders, ran into his room,
collected his gun, and made off. He sprinted across seven lands
and seven seas till he reached the celebrated Forest of Reincarnation.
He breathed a sigh of relief that he should have arrived before
sunrise when, according to Ejima's declaration seventeen years
ago, she would be coming here to rejoin her sister for their return
journey to the sun. He could see from the breaking glow in the
eastern sky that the sun was just about to emerge. He climbed
the huge tree, hid at the spot he now knew so well, and waited.
He could see in the distance that Ejima's sister was already back
and was waiting in the boat. She was as beautiful as ever and
hummed the most melodious tune the hunter had ever heard.

Soon enough, the hunter heard footsteps coming through

103

the forest. He looked up and saw that the sun had just risen on the horizon. At that moment Ejima emerged, walking like a queen in a fairy tale, as nude and beautiful as she was when he first saw her seventeen years ago. The hunter took a deep breath.

'Stop where you are!' he roared and jumped down the tree.

Ejima was so startled that she nearly fell to the ground. And recognizing the hunter, she began to tremble with fear. Her face became paler than pale and her heart almost stopped beating.

'Brave Hunter, Brave Hunter,' she called, 'what do you want with me?'

'You knew the answer to that question before you asked it, Ejima,' he answered; 'I promised myself to make you my wife. I can disappoint anyone but myself.'

'But this cannot be, Brave Hunter. I do not belong to your world. I was only there on holiday. I belong to the sun.'

'I know that, Ejima. That's why I'm here to prevent you going back to the sun. You must come back with me to my world.'

'And if I do not come?'

'I will shoot you dead like a bird.'

'But if you do that, I am doomed. I will belong to neither the world of men nor the sun. And I shall never rejoin my sister again.'

'I know that, Ejima, very well. Just as I know that you will not be foolish enough to inflict such an eternal curse upon your soul.'

Ejima burst into tears.

'Brave Hunter, Brave Hunter,' she cried. 'Please let me go to my sister. Take pity on us both and let us return to the sun. We'll make you the richest man in the world and give you anything you want.'

'The only thing I want from life is love and a cure from boredom. I know you can give me both. Can't you see it is either your freedom or mine? And my hunting instinct says to me: don't forget the rules.'

104

Ejima realized that pleading till doomsday would not move the hunter.

'All right, Brave Hunter,' she said, looking into his eyes for the first time in their experience. 'I'll marry you and make you the most loving of wives. Meanwhile, run back to my parents' house at Okija. You'll find my corpse lying in the coffin, surrounded by mourners. Tell my parents that they had made a dreadful mistake, that I was not dead, just temporarily unconscious. Then slap me seven times on each cheek and ask me to arise. You will see what will happen then.'

'Yes,' replied the Hunter, 'but to make sure that what I want to happen will indeed happen, lend me a lock of your hair, will you?'

'But why?'

'Because I know you cannot go back to the sun imperfect.'

'But how do you know these things?' asked Ejima.

'Maybe I myself was once a son of the sun.'

The hunter took a lock off Ejima's hair and departed. He went to the funeral scene at Okija and did as he had been told. Ejima got out of the coffin, asking, to the stupefied delight of all present, what the fuss was all about. Six months later she was married to the hunter, and nine months after that she gave birth to a daughter. Everyone commented on how alike mother and daughter looked, just like identical twins, but members of the family kept their secret to themselves. They had no more children and lived happily to ripe old age. When death came at last, they all went back to the sun where you can still see them taking their evening strolls, hand in hand. Now, my good stranger, you know what makes the sunset so beautiful: the glowing beauty of the daughters of the sun.'

When the old lady finished her tale, she exposed her toothless gums in a warm smile and poked her companion with her walking stick.

'Now, what do you think of it, eh?'

105

'It's a lovely story, Great Lady,' replied the man carrying the pot. 'I have heard many legends in my time but your story makes children's stories of them all. When did you say it happened?'

'Oh, many many years ago, when men were men and women were women, when maids had breasts and stayed pretty as nature made them, when men, like giants, were so wrapped in muscles and so proud of this that they dared not hide their thighs in cotton as they do today, it was then, my dear stranger, that such things as you have just heard could happen.'

Not only were her words the same as at the beginning of her story, but her pauses, gestures, and voice inflexions were no different. It was obvious she had repeated this tale many times before. The tall stranger smiled understandingly.

'In this day and age,' he muttered to himself, 'when kindness is so rare, why should a helpless old lady not invent some little tale with which to amuse people whom she tricks into carrying her water-pot home for her?'

'Did you say something?' asked the old woman. 'I'm half deaf.'

'No, Great Lady, nothing at all,' he said with a smile. He was contented that the day had not passed in vain. Yes, he had collected a legend, he thought. And the legend was not the story he heard, but the lady who told it, an old woman who, taken unawares by an era when everything had cash value, had risen above the level of charity by converting her lively imagination into practical currency. No one would accuse her of not paying for her water labour. Least of all, her conscience.